ABOUT PROSE

"The tone is personal and intimate in a way that effectively bonds author and reader together, so that reading this book becomes a life-enhancing experience.

This eclectic mix of memories of shared love, laughter, and hope should appeal to a wide readership, and deserves to find a place in every public library collection.

Most of the tales can be seen as 'memoirs in miniature,' possessing an immediacy and a realism that is appealing in its authenticity."

Lois C. Henderson, in the New York Journal of Books:
www.nyjournalofbooks.com

Sharing
enjoy !
peneda

Prose To Go

Tales From A Private List

Edited by

Irene Davis
Fred Desjardins
Barbara Florio-Graham

Writers make the world seem coherent.
They decipher babble;
they banish ambiguity and fluff;
they amuse;
they persuade;
they convince;
they entice;
they inform.
Writers make the world seem coherent.

(Lawrence Jackson, 1942-1998, Past President of PWAC)

Bridgeross Communications

Library and Archives Canada Cataloguing in Publication

Prose to go : tales from a private list / edited by Irene Davis, Fred

Desjardins, Barbara Florio-Graham.

ISBN 978-0-9866522-1-9

1. Canadian literature (English)--21st century. I. Davis, Irene, 1932-
II. Desjardins, Fred, 1952- III. Graham, Barbara Florio, 1934-

PS8251.1.P76 2011   C810.8'006   C2011-901756-3

First Published in 2011 by Bridgeross Communications
Dundas, Ontario, Canada

4

Table of Contents

WHAT IN THE WORLD 75

Acknowledgments

Editorial Team
Primary Editor: Irene Davis
Acquisitions Editor: Fred Desjardins
Managing Editor: Barbara Florio-Graham

Design Team
Concept: Barbara Florio-Graham and Steve Pitt
Execution: Julie and John Watson
Technical Advisor: Luigi Benetton
Cover photo by Steve Pitt

Stories in this anthology were originally published in:
The Bloor West Villager
The Christian Science Monitor
The Concordia University Alumni Magazine
CURRENT: Spina Bifida & Hydrocephalus Association of
Ontario
EMMY Magazine
The Guardian
The Globe and Mail
The Jewish Magazine
The Kings County Record
Laugh Your Shorts Off (published by Writers In Residence)
http://lifeasahuman.com
The London Free Press
The Ottawa Citizen
The Peterborough Examiner
Stitches
Today's Seniors

Foreword

by Barbara Florio-Graham

We range in age over four decades, have degrees in such varied disciplines as engineering, economics and criminology (in addition to English and journalism). We are Christians and Jews, atheists and agnostics. We are single, married with young children, married without any children, divorced, grandparents, and sons and daughters of elderly parents.

We admit to being addicted to writing.

This group was formed in August, 2007, when I created a Private List with two dozen friends I'd gotten to know during 29 years of membership in the Professional Writers' Association of Canada.

Our diversity has turned out to be one of the strengths of the list. Whether one of us describes something annoying or tragic, there is at least one other person who has dealt with the problem and is able to offer practical suggestions, empathy, or comfort.

Professional writers who have written dozens of books and contributed to hundreds of magazines, newspapers and websites, we share news and information about writing. But we also voice our opinions about things in the news and in our private lives.

Our close friendship has allowed us to take wildly different views on many issues, including ethics and religion, with civility and grace. Our messages reflect our beliefs, but also elation, depression, frustration and grief.

This compilation is just a sampling from this group of 23 talented professionals. The bios at the back of the book acknowledge specific contributors to this volume, but all members of the list appear below.

Barbara (Bobbi) Florio-Graham

Bobbi's Private List

Elle Andra-Warner, Thunder Bay, Ontario:
http://www.andra-warner.com/
Lorri Benedik, Montreal, Quebec: lorri@lorribenedik.com
Luigi Benetton, Toronto, Ontario: www.LuigiBenetton.com
Lanny Boutin, Gibbons, Alberta: http://lannyboutin.com/
Joanne Carnegie, Montreal, Quebec; www.writers.ca
Irene Davis, Toronto, Ontario: www.writers.ca
Fred Desjardins, Halifax, Nova Scotia: www.fdesjardins.com
Barbara Florio-Graham, Gatineau, Quebec:
www.SimonTeakettle.com
Trudy Kelly Forsythe, Hampton, New Brunswick:
www.trudykellyforsythe.com
Debbie Gamble, Alexandra, Prince Edward Island
Gordon Gibb, Peterborough, Ontario: www.GordonGibb.com
Kathleen Hamilton, Montreal, Quebec:
www.truenorthcrosswords.com

Hélèna Katz, Fort Smith, Northwest Territories:
www.katzcommunications.ca
Mark Kearney, London, Ontario: www.triviaguys.com
Dale Kerr, Sutton West, Ontario: www.grgbuilding.com
Helen Lammers-Helps, New Dundee, Ontario
Barbara Bunce Desmeules Massobrio, Montreal, Quebec:
www.travellingbooky.com
Fred McEvoy, Ottawa, Ontario
Lorna Olson, Thunder Bay, Ontario
Steve Pitt, North Bay, Ontario: http://stevepitt.ca
Julie Watson, Charlottetown, Prince Edward Island:
www.seacroftpei.com
Kevin Yarr, Charlottetown, Prince Edward Island:
http://tinyurl.com/255njuv
Hilda Young, Petawawa, Ontario:
http://hildaleapsforward.blogspot.com

Misadventures

Driving Alpacas

by Hélèna Katz

The rumor around Fort Smith, the town of 2,300 people where we live in the Northwest Territories, was that we had gone off the road and into a swamp, the truck had flipped and we had all died. They had it sort of right. Except for the part about the truck flipping. And we're not dead. In fact, we all escaped miraculously without a scratch.

It all started when my partner, Mike, decided to bring up some alpacas and llamas to the Northwest Territories. With their woolly coats and their roots in the chilly Andean mountains of Peru, the animals seemed well equipped for life in the North. He bought six alpacas and two llamas from a farm in Salmon Arm, British Columbia. At the end of June, he, his friends Tim and Ann, and I drove down to pick up the woolly brood. The three drivers would take turns at the wheel during what we anticipated would be a 21-hour journey.

Things were going quite smoothly on the drive back up to Fort Smith. We were making good time, and the animals seemed to be good travelers for the most part—lying down in the trailer while we drove and standing up when we took breaks from the road. The two llamas and four male alpacas were together in the back of the trailer. The female and a cria (a young alpaca) were in a separate compartment at the front. Females and males need to be kept separate for obvious reasons and young males don't hang out with the big boys until they're about two years old because they'll get bullied.

Morgan, the baby, happily chowed down on the bale of hay hanging from a hay bag on the wall. The boys in the back nibbled on hay that was spread out on the floor. Pumpkin, one of the llamas, often poked his head out the window of the trailer to see what was happening. Since the alpacas were too small to reach up and get the view, we wondered if Pumpkin had been appointed by the other animals to look outside and report back on what was happening beyond the tin can on wheels.

Bee Jay, a black alpaca, was quickly nicknamed *Goober* because he had the green telltale signs of having been spat on by another alpaca. It didn't take long to figure out who was using him as a spittoon. Blue, the smallest but most dominant of the males, had his lower lip hanging down as though he had just had a shot of novocaine. Call it the post-spit position.

Then the sun went down and so did our luck. We just barely coasted into Peace River in northern Alberta on our last bit of diesel. The guys at the Tim Horton's were great. It was 11 pm. and they had just closed, but reopened so that we could empty our bladders and refill our thermos jugs with coffee.

Then the hunt for diesel began. The guy at the Shell station, who had just closed up, stared without any sympathy through the glass at our pitiful, begging faces. I momentarily contemplated raising my shirt and flashing him, but then realized I probably didn't have persuasive merchandise.

The only 24-hour gas station in town had gas but not the much-needed diesel. The idea of staying overnight in a town full of over-caffeinated cowboys didn't appeal to us. More than an hour and $60 later, a guy showed up with a jerrycan of diesel and we were on our way. We filled up on truck fuel in Grimshaw and human fuel in High Level.

The next thing we all remember is waking up to Ann screaming beside me in the backseat as the truck and trailer went off the road and plopped into a swamp. Everyone in the truck had fallen asleep, including the driver. Amazingly we all emerged from the accident without a scratch.

We waited an hour for the tow truck driver to come from High Level. I earned brownie points for being brave enough (or dumb enough, depending on your perspective) to go into the mosquito-infested bush to answer Mother Nature's call—twice. Eventually the tow truck pulled us back onto the road with about as much ease as we had slid into the swamp in the first place.

We unloaded the animals into the pasture when we got home. Alas, the misadventures continued. The boys managed to knock down a temporary gate between them and the pen where Carmen and the cria were. Bee Jay, undoubtedly sensing an opportunity to pick on someone smaller, chased the cria around until Mike was able to separate them.

The bugs here have voracious appetites, probably due to the short chomping season. The animals were getting bitten, so the town animal shelter folks stopped by and helped Mike put the gang in the garage and workshop with some hay. For the first time since we had left Salmon Arm two days earlier, Ghost (one of the alpacas) stopped complaining about being homesick.

Three days after we got here, Mike, Ann and Larry drove the brood down to a farm north of Grande Prairie to board the animals until bug season was over and the barn was built. As Ann quipped when the animals happily climbed back into the metal llama limo: *They're probably thinking, Oh good! Our holiday in hell is finally over.*

This story was first published in http://lifeasahuman.com

Well Seated

by Lanny Boutin

Unlike children, most cats I've known have happily given up the active life by the age of three, content to eat the same food every day, and not needing five books, two stuffed animals and constant adult companionship to use the washroom.

I knew having kids would be harder than cats, but in hindsight, I really wish they were born with whiskers.

Cats use their whiskers as measuring sticks to keep them from getting stuck in tight spaces. The whiskers touch the sides, the cat retreats. For a cat it's that simple.

With kids nothing is simple.

Take the boy in my town who spent an hour roasting in the hot summer sun, his head jammed between the rails of a black metal church fence, his backside pointed out towards the busy street. The rails had to be pried apart to free him.

Or my little cousin who slipped his head through the hand carved imported wooden railing on the top floor of the rotunda in the Alberta Legislative Building; a rather hysterical caretaker repeatedly assured us he would not cut the bars. Luckily, the boy's head finally slipped back out.

Or my son and the toilet seat.

We had just moved to a new house, in a new neighborhood. I was in the basement unpacking boxes when I heard those dreaded words, *Mom, I'm stuck.*

There standing before me was my three-year-old son, with a new, kid size, white plastic toilet seat draped around his neck like a collar.

Now there are times when the hardest part of being a parent is not laughing and this was one of them. Looking into those terrified blue eyes quickly wiped the smile from my face. I knew I had a problem.

It might seem like a simple thing to remove a toilet seat from around a toddler's neck; what goes on, must come off, right? But the wizard who invented this particular toilet seat designed it with a beveled edge so it would lock securely onto an adult seat. And my dear son had managed to pull it on upside down, so the beveled edge was now resting under his ears. His big red swollen ears: swollen from what I guessed were his own numerous attempts to pry off the seat.

Cutting it was futile. All the tools were packed in hundreds of poorly marked boxes in the garage. The only thing I had in the house was a pair of kitchen scissors and a pair of long-retired wire cutters. Neither even scratched the surface.

And even though my son wasn't in pain or physical danger, I could see that leaving him in the seat would make dressing him a bit of a challenge.

I don't really think the phone company anticipated this one when they jingled, *let your fingers do the walking,* but my options were running dry.

The nurse at the hospital suggested a hacksaw. Ours was still packed, which of course was a good thing. I didn't think my son would have let a woman who had once sawed into her big toe while trimming the corner off a shelf come near him with such a weapon of destruction.

Even if she was his mother.

It took a few minutes but the man at the ambulance authority was finally able to stifle his laughter long enough to give me the non-emergency number for the fire department. They assured me they weren't busy and would be happy to pop over and have a look.

As I put down the receiver, I heard the sirens. Soon the lights of the approaching trucks lit up the night, as two enormous red fire trucks screeched to a halt in front of my house. My son and my daughter, who was two at the time, watched in awe as eight fully outfitted firefighters, carrying large florescent orange emergency medical kits, thundered up our stairs and into our living room.

Both children grabbed the back of one of my legs and started to scream.

It took 5 minutes to convince my son to show them the seat. And a detailed tour of all their equipment before he would let them touch it. It took less than three seconds for a large pair of tin snips to slice thought the plastic. He was free.

For a long time afterwards, each time we heard sirens my son wondered aloud if another little boy's head was stuck in a toilet seat.

I dearly hoped the episode would teach him a lesson, but as I bandage his baby finger, the one which he cut as we pried his hand from the hole in the library counter, I wonder.

This story was first published in the Christian Science Monitor

Just Desserts

by Joanne Carnegie

When he was eight, my son developed the habit of storing his lunchtime rejects in his backpack.

Of course he never told me his lunch wasn't up to the mark: I was a single mom, up at dawn denaturing vegetables and peeling plastic from cheese slices the texture of silly-putty. Still, he could have ditched his cucumber sandwiches at school, like a normal kid, or fed them to the neighbor's dog. But I think he thought the neighbor would rat him out, and he knew the gorgons patrolling the lunch room would extract his teeth, one by one, if he dumped his celery sticks there instead of air-freighting them to the starving Ethiopians.

What he did instead was carry the stuff around in his backpack for weeks, hermetically sealed in plastic, thanks to the modern re-sealable sandwich bag. Luckily, he was in a mostly vegetarian phase, which saved him from being attacked by buzzards en route to the school bus.

But this also meant his ruse went undetected for quite some time. His cellulose graveyard remained a secret until I went into his backpack to look for a permission slip. At the bottom of his bag was a mini-archeological site, a carefully layered collection of several weeks' worth of motherly offerings.

Lord knows what he was planning to do with the stuff. Something noble, I'm sure: perhaps he was running an old-age home for forlorn food, or maybe he planned to use his stash as projectiles, in the event of a home invasion.

(Doctor to nurse in emergency room, over body of foiled thief: *Patient has severe fruit contusions with multiple dried baloney wounds and aggravated bran muffin abrasions.*)

It's crucial to handle these child-rearing dilemmas properly. So I yelled: *What the bloody hell were you thinking?* Then I lectured him on nutrition and the evils of wasting my labor. Hammering home the point, I ordered him not to keep his leftovers in his backpack. He nodded. Problem solved!

Daily inspections for the next few weeks revealed a backpack as tidy as a locker at boot camp. So I carried on carving smiley faces into radishes and, wanting to please as well as demonstrate the value of compromising, bought spongy brown bread to cut into the shape of gingerbread men.

Then came the ants. One day my son approached me and said, in a small-child whimper: *Mommy, my floor's moving!*

It was an odd comment. I smelled his breath to see if he'd gotten into the liquor cabinet, then went to his room to see what was up.

He stayed at the doorway while I went in. At first I saw nothing. Then gradually I began to sense movement, a ragged line of little white dots heading for the corner. Barely visible against the mottled grey of his carpet were squadrons of tiny ants engaged in complicated tactical maneuvers with scores of crumbs. They'd come trooping in through a crack in the basement, drawn by the aroma of antique sandwiches and festering fruit. The mind of an ant is not mysterious.

These ones must have been delirious with joy. Behind a bookshelf in my son's room was a treasure trove of curling sandwich fragments, rotting fruit, and tightly-sealed sandwich bags filled with pale grey liquid and a surprising quantity of seeds. Some of the bags contained what appeared to be dark primal ooze. Luckily, none of the bags had leaked.

Drawing upon the instincts of Grade Three logic, my son refused to enter his bedroom until I got rid of the ants. Apparently, bugs are gross, but food on the fast track to the afterlife—hey, what's your problem?

Twenty-four hours and a handful of ant traps later, the invaders were gone, and the coast was clear.

Until the mice.

The ants and I had overlooked a second pile of abandoned lunch offerings, artfully concealed under a rarely-worn bicycle helmet stashed under the bed. It was easy to determine who the intruders were: mice leave their calling cards.

I asked my son where the food had come from. He thought for a moment, then said, *I don't know.*

But, he added, with big, serious eyes, *If any more turns up, I'll let you know.*

Later that week, to celebrate our victory over the fur-covered Visigoths, I made rice pudding for dessert, with currants instead of the usual raisins. Between mouthfuls, my son asked why the pudding tasted so different. *Oh!* I said, as he smacked his lips over the last morsel, *I think some mouse turds fell into the pot.*

His room's been as clean as a licked spoon ever since.

##

August Anxiety

by Steve Pitt

Hey, Old Man. Can I have the computer for a bit? asks my 17-year-old son, Kevin. More of a demand, really, but that's all right. For only one more day, we will be a one computer family and then someone from a company called The Geek Chorus will be coming over to install something called a wireless router and my wife, my son and I will never have to share a computer again. Instead, we will all split off to our separate work stations in different rooms of the house and do our own things. Hopefully, we will still come together for holiday meals at least twice a year.

Pitt-the-Younger's timing is actually perfect. I've been up since 5 a.m. trying to make a writing deadline. I'm into the homestretch but I'm burned. I need my power nap. I stand up and we do the computer station shuffle: each of us trying to maneuvre around the other in this cramped basement corner. Gawd, he's huge, I think for the 'illionth time. Now six-three, a sinewy 190 pounds against my five-eight and let's-not-go-there-mass.

I stretch out on the couch on the far side of the room and fall asleep to the tic-tic-bac! of my son's fingers mosh-pitting on computer keys, his head bobbing to the muted strains of Cannibal Corpse escaping from his headphones as he checks in with his friends around the world. I drift away and a familiar sense of panic takes over. I'm having another anxiety dream. It's August.

When I was an armored truck guard, I used to get anxiety dreams about being shot at but when I reached for my holster I'd find my .38 special replaced by a banana (no Freudian analysis, please). When I was studying to be a minister, I used to get dreams where I was about to preach a sermon to a packed church and I'd open my bible only to find my underlined Ecclesiastes quotes gone.

Every year, since I became a stay-at-home dad, I've had recurring dreams where I am trying to get my toddler-age son to school, only my car won't start, the neighbors won't stop and the buses all veer off in the wrong direction. When finally we do make it to the school we find that the doors are all locked, and as we stand outside I can actually hear the principal's voice saying on the school intercom, *You must be some kind of lousy parent if you can't even get your kid here on time for the first day of school...*

It doesn't matter what age my son is in real time. In my dreams he is always a toddler. Unpleasant hits of reality sometimes intrude. I'm always an older and fatter version of me but my son is still just a tyke, dressed in fresh pressed matching First-Day-of-School Speedy Gonzales shorts and t-shirt. Again, the car doesn't start. The neighbors pass us by as we wave frantically from the sidewalk. We catch a bus, only to have it inexplicably turn around and head in the opposite direction it is supposed to go.

The anxiety nightmare seems to go on for hours. We change buses. We try cabs. We run up and down streets that are simultaneously familiar and bizarrely foreign. I keep promising my son that we are almost there only to be proven a liar over and over again. Each time, my son just looks up at me, nods and smiles with implicit trust despite my incessant incompetence. Then, by divine miracle, we are in the school yard. But this time, kids and parents are still calmly standing out front. We've made it!

I suddenly realize two things. One, this time I knew the school door was going to open. Two, I realize that this was just another dream and I am about to wake up on the basement couch, probably face-to-face with the arse end of the family pooch, who likes to sneak up and reverse spoon beside me when I'm sleeping.

In other dreams, when I realize that I'm only dreaming, I know I have a few seconds to do any crazy thing I feel like. I can step off rooftops and fly. I can win shoot-outs with a .38 Special banana or moon a church full of the faithful and still make a killing on the collection plate.

The school bell rings; Kevin is about to walk toward those open doors but before he can I snatch him up in a bear hug, close my eyes and hang on trying to hold back the tears. As much as I adore my grown up son, I desperately miss my smiling child who would follow his fallible old man anywhere. For one glorious dream moment I have my little boy back – until I hear my adult son's voice tell me *Hey, Old Man. You're scaring the dog.*

##

My Magnificent Impression

by Gordon Gibb

It was a great suit, as suits go. A three-piece suit, grey in colour with pinstripes and matching pants. My impressive, practical suit, ordered on sale from the Sears catalogue just days before my big trip to the city.

Big trips to the city are important to a young man with a young family and an equally young career. A career in need of a kick to the next plateau, with a more impressive paycheck to go with it. So when the opportunity came to drive to Toronto to meet with an important supplier, I wanted to look my best.

I wanted to make an impression.

And so the day dawned when I donned my new suit, and bidding my young wife goodbye, slid behind the wheel of our old car for the two-hour drive to the city.

But first I needed gas, and on a blustery day in winter the *We-Serve* lane was choked with motorists eager to stay in from the cold. It wasn't that cold, really. But people get lazy sometimes.

The self-serve lane was empty. Anything but lazy and not wanting to be late, for arriving late would leave anything but a good impression, I wheeled into the self-serve lane, grabbed the hose and pumped away in the manner to which

I am accustomed. Full bore. I was on my way to an important appointment in the city. And I was a young man in a suit with career advancement on his mind.

That's when the old car decided it had had enough of my suit and my gas, and it belched. Regurgitate is a more fitting verb, and it did so all over my pants, delivering a soaker that migrated right into my shoes.

There I was, dressed to the nines and smelling like a refinery, with no time to change and nothing to change into. I thought about lighting a match. A fireball would be a good excuse. People would believe a fireball. But there were no matches. I didn't smoke. But I sure smelled.

And so I pressed on, down the 401 to the big city of Toronto, drying my pants with the heat on high—which also describes my state of mind from the fumes, when I finally parked the car on Adelaide Street for my 10 o'clock appointment. At least my pants were dry, and the smell had dissipated, too. Or so I thought. A dozen turned-up noses in the elevator confirmed my suspicion that gas smells just as bad when it's dry, as when it isn't.

Eleven floors later my host greeted me graciously. *How was the drive?* he queried. *Fine,* says I. And then, the uncomfortable pause that happens when somebody notices something but doesn't wish to ask, and the other somebody doesn't know whether to say, or how to say, and therefore says nothing at all.

Would you like a tour, and meet the staff?

Boy, would I.

Later, it was lunch—at a quaint bistro just around the corner. A delightful little place, known for its intimate ambience and selection of wines, although I suspect everyone's palate was just a little off that day. Someone remarked to their waiter that the plants seemed to be wilting. We didn't stay for dessert.

Why I didn't bolt then and there I'll never know, for there were more tours, and handshakes and intimate huddles. And then, mercifully, it was time to leave. Bidding my genteel host goodbye, who smiled politely and said it was a (sniff) pleasure, I went down to fetch my car.

Which wasn't there. I had parked in a no-parking zone under a sign I had failed to see, towed to the city pound and held ransom for seventy dollars.

I didn't have seventy dollars.

Nor did I have a credit card, a debit card, a checkbook or a quarter to call home. But I did have my paycheck in my wallet, and a sympathetic host 11 floors above.

And so back up the elevator I go, back into the posh lobby that now smelled of air freshener, with no money and no car, but with an uncashed paycheck and a fetching three-piece suit that smelled like Dad's carburetor on the kitchen table.

And after taking me to his own bank and personally vouching for my identity, my long-suffering host hailed me a cab and with cash in hand I was off to rescue my car, and what remained of my dignity.

Later that night, with my car in the drive and my suit in the garage, I shared my day with my young wife and some equally young wine.

Look on the bright side, she says. *You did what you set out to do.*

You made an impression.

This story was first published in The Peterborough Examiner

Silence Is Not Golden

by Irene Davis

At this writing my laryngitis is four weeks old and still going strong.

You've heard of three-alarm fires; this is a three-doctor case—one G.P. and two specialists. I may yet end up in the Guinness Book of Records.

If you've never suffered a protracted case of no-voice-it-is let me enlighten you as to the problems that ensue.

There's the need to be a good sport, to maintain a smiling front while inside, teeth are gritted and patience sorely tried. That front is fading fast; I will probably slug the next person who says playfully to my husband, *Hey this is great for you, so quiet!* Or how about the ones who just burst out laughing? If I were playing Freud, I'd say that unconsciously we don't want to have to listen, so hey ain't it great when someone can't talk.

There's the struggle to communicate. Those whispers I really shouldn't inflict on my strained vocal cords—and that no one can hear anyway. Endless scribbling on my magic slate—which no one can read because my thoughts spill out so fast the writing degenerates into a scrawl. Snapping my fingers, pounding on a table, the floor, anything, to get attention—then trying to convey my message. My husband's left arm is turning a nice shade of blue, and he's beginning to eye me warily and inch away when I approach.

And then there's the telephone. Ignore it or answer it—disaster lurks either way. Shopping—if a transaction takes more than a pointing finger and a nod of the head, forget it. Dental appointments—try to explain what the problem is.

There's aerobics class—not too bad during class, everyone is too busy getting that heartbeat up to talk. But afterwards! Feeling even more defenseless in my unclothed state, I contribute nods of wisdom to the whirlpool conversation.

Even a walk in the neighborhood has its hazards. Casual acquaintances greet me, then, as the import of my smiles and waves sinks in, burst into a torrent of questions.

Can't you talk? How long have you had that? What did the doctor say? etc., etc., etc.

I have developed a good imitation of the Gallic shrug.

Restaurants are something else. I jab my finger at various spots on the menu. With a puzzled look the hovering waiter tries to follow the finger, as my companion, ever helpful, says, *She can't talk.* Alternatively, I sit there with a smile on my face as my companion gives my order. *She wants coffee and a cheese sandwich.* The waiter either eyes me dubiously or throws me a *don't worry dear I'll look after you* smile.

The conversation sparkles. I fill up endless scraps of paper, which my companion dutifully reads before launching into a monologue or lapsing into silence. When we leave, we carefully gather up our conversation and put it with the trash.

Several weeks of this, and believe me, you've lost the funny side. You begin to wonder whether you're doomed to go on forever, whispering and scribbling and pounding and pointing.

And you long for the sound of a human voice—yours.

##

Lobster

by Julie V. Watson

Appearing on television is intimidating to *newbies,* and on one unforgettable occasion for me, proved terrifying.

In my job promoting shellfish from Prince Edward Island, I found myself suddenly thrust into the small screen foray. Me, an untrained, horribly audience-shy, beginner. I drew on an earlier experience with media for strength. It had happened in Vancouver when I was on the opposite coast to promote Prince Edward Island mussels. A rank newcomer to the food celebrity scene, I was a bundle of nerves as I was escorted down to Vicki Gabereau's tiny basement studio at CBC Radio Vancouver. The woman I thought of as the Queen of Radio turned out to be just like other folk, but more fun. We talked. We shared thoughts. We enjoyed each other's opinions. There just happened to be a microphone hanging between us that carried our conversation to listeners.

I realized then that people who interview are almost always nice—almost ordinary, even TV folks hidden behind makeup so thick it would take a knife to scrape it off. I learned listeners enjoyed conversations and I stopped worrying. With that attitude I quickly overcame my fear when we started the live-TV remote with a news show in Calgary.

I was in Charlottetown, Prince Edward Island, on opening day of the lobster season, charged with showing viewers out west how to crack and eat a lobster. One earpiece connected me with the TV host so that I could do a Show and Tell. In the other ear I could hear the producer or director—someone giving me curt instructions. The sun was shining on the harbor behind me, spring was in the air, and I was about to enjoy my first lobster of the season. Even with the bossy voice telling me to tilt the claw towards the camera, or to hold it *right there* for a second, I was bouncing with enthusiasm.

A twist to break my lobster and the show began with much fun and laughter. I was using a spoon and nutcrackers, no fancy lobster crackin' tools, to show how simple it was to enjoy lobster in the shell. Suddenly I felt a sting on the palm of my hand. A quick glance down made my heart jump. I had cut my hand on an edge of shell, or one of the sharp spines. I was bleeding like the proverbial stuck pig.

So there I was, holding my hand back so that no one would see the blood literally streaming from my palm while I was taking the lobster apart and eating it. I tried keeping my hand in my lap, but cracking the shell with just my left hand was like playing two violins at the same time.

So now the producer guy is barking in one ear, *Turn the lobster, do this, do that*. The host is asking me to show them more of the meat and shell—all nigh impossible because the

41

last message I wanted to send was that eating lobster from the shell is dangerous. I would have lost my job!

And so, relying on the lessons I'd learned with Vicki Gabereau, I just kept rattling on, stuffing lobster meat in my mouth and going *Mmmmmm* a lot. At the end the host did a great job of winding up the piece, joking about how much meat there was in the lobster, etc. I had impressed myself because I kept my cool and didn't freak.

Finally, it was just me and the producer guy yakking in my ear. He ranted and raved until I turned my hand over so he saw my palm and I tipped the plate up so he could see the blood. No apologies but at least the ranting stopped. As is the case with TV they quickly moved on to the next segment. The camera man left. The restaurant staff concerned themselves with rescuing the table cloth and mopping up the floor. So there I was on my own, wondering if I should drive myself to the ER. Celebrity status can be so fleeting!

I did quite a few more TV spots demonstrating how to eat a lobster but learned to ask if we could tape. Never cut myself again.

##

Rear-View Mirror

Places Of The Heart

by Irene Davis

There are places that dwell within us, places of the heart.

Sometimes those places exist now only in memory. Peopled by the ghosts of those once loved, they can be a haven now and then, and a bridge between relationships past and present. They also hold and illuminate the one relationship that never goes away—that between I and me.

When you touch one of my special places, you touch me, and we too relate. Come with me now to the Kensington of my childhood, in Toronto, circa 1940, peopled with babushkaed women laden with shopping bags, children darting around hydrants and between legs, smiling old men in crumpled suits.

That one! says my grandmother, and the bearded, skull-capped man reaches into the cage standing on the sidewalk and grabs a protesting chicken by its spindly legs. Holding tight to the wildly-flapping soup-destined squawk-box, feathers flying behind, we push past the chickens and ducks, past the oranges and bananas, past the steel racks holding the shirts-too-small and pants-too-long, to the ritual slaughterer. Later would come the slow, painful job of de-feathering and cleaning, and the bird's final, pristine appearance on the Sabbath-eve table.

Later too, would come my grandfather, fresh from synagogue, with a smile for me and a kiss for my grandmother—*my queen*. Dinner on the whiter-than-white tablecloth, Sabbath candles glowing, flickering.

Now my hand feels warm inside my grandmother's. The guttural friendliness of Yiddish sounds in my ears.

Sholom Aleichem—peace be with you; hello, how are you?

Aleichem Sholom—and with you, peace; so-so, could be worse, can't complain.

On to the fishmarket.

The yellow sawdust slithers under my feet. The sea-smell of herring is sharp in my nose. In the window the huge slab of lox lies pink and tender in the sun. The flies like it too, and are brushed away by an impatient hand before the long blade sinks into the slab. Thin pink slices peel off the knife—thinner and faster than any mechanical slicer could manage, mouthwatering salty morsels waiting to be sandwiched with bagel and cheese.

To the baker now, and for me a chocolate eclair supreme. Real, drippy chocolate surrounding fresh whipped cream, delicate pastry between. Crunchy and melting, sweet stickiness everywhere. I lick my fingers. Time to move on.

I am reluctant now to leave this Kensington of mine; this place to which I can retreat from time to time, to touch once again my roots.

It joins those I once loved with those I love now, me in-between, my arms stretched across the generations.

Through it, the I that has become can communicate with the me that was then, to gain greater understanding of where I have been and where I am going, and what my hopes are for those who come after me.

For me, this place—and other such places of the heart—is home base. I reach for it now and then, stroke it with a gentle touch, remembering. And then I smile and return to living.

Time, indeed, to move on.

This story was first published in The Jewish Magazine

The North Becomes Her

by Hélèna Katz

It was autumn in the Yukon and I was walking along the edge of the Dempster Highway, about 60 miles north of Dawson City. This gravel road wends its way for 442 miles up to Inuvik in the Northwest Territories. It's a place where few cars pass and even fewer amenities are available. The vivid reds, yellows and oranges of the tundra in fall colors framed the road. Tiny trees and lichen looked like a carefully woven tapestry. I stopped for a moment and looked down the road towards the place where the land meets the sky. A powerful sensation suddenly rose up from the ground and my feet, traveling up through my body. In that instant, I felt the power and force of nature and a deep connection with the land. I was a part of nature—at one with the land.

I returned home to Montreal, the place where I was born and raised. But the North never left me. I kept looking for excuses to return. I came up with a masters' thesis topic that took me north again in fall 2003, this time to Hay River, a community of 3,600 in the southern Northwest Territories. I met Mike in July 2004 when I went to nearby Fort Smith to research a travel story about Wood Buffalo National Park.

We kept in touch. Our first date, in February 2006, was an expensive affair. Forget the wine, flowers and romantic weekend. During Mike's eight-hour drive down to Fort

McMurray to meet me, his truck slid on some ice on the winter road and scraped the bark off a tree. The cracked windshield was replaced in Fort McMurray and the dented passenger door was straightened out in Hay River. Between the repairs, gas and hotel in Fort Chipewyan, the bill for that date was more than $4,000.

First I fell in love with the North; then I fell in love with a Northerner. After spending five months subsidizing hotels, airlines and gas stations, I moved from downtown Montreal to the outskirts of Fort Smith in July 2006 to be with Mike. This pretty town of about 2,400 people sits on the banks of the Slave River, just a stone's throw from the Alberta border. Residents are a mix of non-Natives, Chipewyan and Cree from the Salt River First Nation and Smith's Landing First Nation.

I moved from a busy neighborhood that had stores galore to a government town with two grocery stores, a pharmacy, a post office, a college, a museum, a Bank of Montreal branch that looks like it's in someone's house, a few shops, a hotel and two restaurants.

Fort Smith is the kind of place where people laugh at you for locking your car, there aren't any traffic lights, and drivers have perfected the art of waving to friends and acquaintances without taking their hand off the steering wheel. When you come off the highway, you hang a right at the main intersection (marked by a four-way stop) if you feel like eating Chinese food and make a left if you want pizza. Even the somebodies are anybodies; my massage therapist is the wife of the MP for the Western Arctic and the former town librarian is married to the deputy premier.

Mike and I live seven miles from town in an area known as Bell Rock. I moved from one of the most densely populated Montreal neighborhoods to a house that is a four-minute walk to the nearest neighbor. We live on three acres of land at the end of a dirt road, and there's nothing but bush behind us. There aren't any sidewalks, the water truck shows up every Thursday morning to replenish our supply, and the septic tank needs to be cleaned out once a year. We also have to cart our own trash to the dump and pick up the mail at the post office because there's no door-to-door delivery.

I miss buttery croissants, Sunday brunch and those little yellow Mexican mangoes bursting with flavor that I loved to buy at fruit stores in my old Mile End neighborhood. But I no longer hear one urban neighbor doing endless renovations while another has a late-night party in their backyard. I have finally found a place that brings me closer to that sense of intimacy with the land I once felt on a quiet stretch of highway in the Yukon.

This story first appeared in http://lifeasahuman.com

Inside The Santa Suit

by Gordon Gibb

I've never had a particular desire to see the world from inside a Santa suit. They can be hot, and the padding confining: any movement might disturb the pillows. And if you're claustrophobic at all, the last place you want to be is stuck behind a huge fake beard reeking of the previous occupant's halitosis, full of minute hairs that tickle your face mercilessly. And you have to SIT there. And sit. And sit some more.

And yet, I have done my time. I have gained that perspective. And every yuletide since, as I make my rounds amidst the mall Santas and mistletoe, my mind goes back to the time when I was in that chair, a child happily perched on my knee, bubbling over with Christmas wishes. Yes, Virginia, I was a Santa Claus.

It was several years ago, when a new mall opened in Peterborough and decided to recruit local celebrities and volunteers to serve as their official mall Santa. We donated our time, while the mall donated Santa's salary to charity. A good idea, we all agreed.

When the call came, I was eager enough to give it a try. I have the big Santa voice. I can Ho Ho Ho with the best of them. But while jolly, I am nowhere near bowlful-of-jelly status. Padding took the form of three pillows, two of which were stuffed down my pants and around my waist, while a third augmented my chest. Right jolly and plump indeed, I thought. That is, until the children bounded up onto the knee of this plump-looking Santa, only to find a thin, scrawny leg. I would prefer to use the term muscular, but you get the idea. Not much bounce there. In hindsight, I must have looked ridiculous.

Our shifts were two hours and we went in armed with a bit of wisdom culled from an experienced colleague. Know the reindeer. Know the child, even if you don't know the name. Never assume a letter exists unless the child brings it up. Never cave in the presence of scepticism. And never, ever, promise. Ever.

I admit to some nervousness the first time I went out to meet my constituents, and my performance was somewhat subdued. My words were few, and my laugh limp and guarded. But with time I gained confidence, and my Ho-Hos grew to be hale and hearty. In spite of the beard reaching up and tickling the inside of my nose, I began to have fun.

The kids can be pretty interesting. Some will treat you like a long-lost friend, talking your ear off about everything they did that year. You have to remind them about their order. Others will quietly state their wish, give you a hug and be off. Some don't say anything, such is their awe. And the odd one will give you the evil eye, the knowing stare that says, ...*I'm onto you, buddy.* This is not a job for the meek.

There are the children of privilege, who sit on my knee dressed to the nines in fashionable winter outerwear, their parents similarly attired, weighted down with packages en route to the Lexus in the parking lot. And on the other end of the scale, the kids who look like they don't have a friend in the world, and not much of anything else, either.

I'll never forget Ginny. She looked to be about eight, sitting on Santa's scrawny knee wearing a dirty blue coat and worn leggings. Her hair was long and unwashed. My impression was that she wasn't kept very well. There was a foot of fresh snow outside, yet she was wearing running shoes. Off in the distance her parents, similarly attired, a couple of dishevelled slobs, both smoking, the guy with a carton of cigarettes under his arm. They were arguing about something. Ginny just looked sad.

I know you've been a very good girl this year, Ginny. I said kindly.

Thank-you, was her reply. Her eyes revealed she had been waiting for this moment all year, and she didn't ever want it to end.

What is your wish, my dear?

Her answer represented something I knew would bring her some warmth and comfort, a smile to her face. Something I knew would elude her. It was the year of Tickle-Me-Elmo, and you couldn't find one to save your life. They had flown off the store shelves, and opportunists were advertising rare finds in the classifieds for hundreds of dollars. She wanted one desperately. But I couldn't promise her one, because somehow I knew she was going to be disappointed. I wanted to say something to comfort her, to give her hope. But what?

My goodness, Ginny, that's a popular one this year.

She smiled. *I know.*

The elves are barely keeping up.

She smiled again. Innocently. Painfully. I was about ready to cry.

Well Ginny, I will try. But can I share a little secret with you?

Sure!

We always like to take a few of the popular toys, and put them aside, tuck them away. A few extras, for those boys and girls who don't have a home, who won't have a Christmas at all.

That's a nice thing to do, Santa.

Yes, Ginny. Some little boys and girls have it really hard. And sometimes Santa has to do something special to help them smile.

Okay.

I think she understood.

You have a lovely smile, Ginny. It's a gift you can give to others, you know...

Really?

Yes.

Merry Christmas, Ginny.

Merry Christmas, Santa, she said quietly.

I'll never know if she found a Tickle-Me-Elmo under her tree that year, the one thing that would have brightened the little girl's gray world. And yet, I can only hope, through her disappointment, she could know that her Tickle-Me-Elmo had gone to a better place, to a kid that really needed it. And I'm hoping that through her tears, she had managed a smile.

Now retired, I still smile when I think of her.

##

This story was first published in The Peterborough Examiner

Now Should Come The Laughter....

by Elle Andra-Warner

Getting born is pretty tough going. They said there would be nothing to it, but leaving my nice, warm, snug home to travel through this murky tunnel makes you think twice about it all. Must be coming to the end as I see a light.

Ah...here I am world, I am born!

Now should come laughter and the congratulatory words of joy. But, wait, something is wrong. Everyone is quiet.

The doctor talks in hushed tones to the nurse and then they both look at me. Is that sadness, maybe a tinge of anger, in their eyes? Hey, come on....why the long, somber faces?

I'm going to give them a few good cries to let them know that I am not pleased with their welcome. No one has even said what a cute baby I am—and aren't all babies supposed to be cute?

A tender voice drifts across the silent room.

Well, doctor, is it a boy or a girl? That soft voice must be my mom.

Hi Mom! I'm here, but no one seems too happy with me.

The doctor looks toward Mom and after a moment's hesitation answers, *Just a minute, I'll check.*

Now, that's a silly thing to say. He should have known that I am a girl the moment I was born. What's going on here?

The doctor finally answers, *It's a girl.*

Doc, how about saying *congratulations* to my mom? You know she had to go through a tough time too.

The voice across the room calls again, but this time there is a hint of fear in it. *Doctor, is there something wrong with the baby?*

Oh-oh...the doctor is walking away from me now. He's going to see my mom.

Hey – what's this nurse doing to me? She's putting a big bandage on my back – I'm certainly not too pleased about that!

This time Mom's voice is more demanding. *Is something wrong? I want to know. What is going on?*

Good for you Mom—make them give us the answer.

The doctor is by Mom's side now. *I'm sorry. Yes, there is something wrong, but you will have to wait until the pediatrician comes and talks to you. I can't tell you any more.*

So, there is something wrong. Gheesh. They sure didn't tell me to get ready for anything like this. I wonder if God knows? Somebody better tell her because I think we're going to need some help!

Mom pressed the doctor, *Why can't you tell me what's wrong with my baby?*

I can't tell you. You will have to wait for the pediatrician.

Has the baby got a finger or toe or something missing?

No, the doctor answers. *There's nothing missing.*

Well, what's wrong? Mom asks.

You'll just have to wait for the pediatrician, the doctor insists, and then leaves the room.

Doctors can be so secretive. What is a *pediatrician* anyway? Why does my mom have to wait for the pediatrician? Why can't this doctor tell my mom? And besides, I want to know pretty quick what this big bandage is doing on my back!

Mom is now talking to the nurse, questioning her. Way to go Mom – we've got a right to know.

Don't tell the doctor I told you, the nurse gently cautions Mom. Then in a hushed, low voice she goes on, though I can barely hear her. *...spina bifida....like a hole in the back...covered with sort of mushing skin.*

I wish the nurse would talk louder. I think she is telling my mom something important.

Can it be fixed? Mom asks.

The room becomes silent again. Why is the nurse taking so long to answer that question? Of course, it can be fixed – can't it? Life certainly seems more complicated already and I'm not even an hour old yet.

The nurse seems to choose her words carefully. *Usually surgery is done as soon as possible to close the back opening. Her legs move fairly well, especially the right one, which is a good sign.*

Well, that sounds a whole lot better. But wait now....does that surgery fix what's wrong with me? And, what does she mean *especially the right one* – what's wrong with my left leg? God, I hope you can hear me because we're definitely going to need some extra assistance here.

Mom says, *Can I hold my baby please?*

The nurse picks me up and gently places me into my mom's arms.

Isn't she a beautiful baby! Mom beams. I had been waiting nine months to hear that. Tears cloud Mom's eyes as her fingers gently caress my eyes, then nose and finally my mouth.

She smiles tenderly at me. *There's going to be some tough times ahead, baby, but hang in.*

Don't worry Mom....we'll make it.

##

This story was first published in CURRENT—publication of the Spina Bifida & Hydrocephalus Association of Ontario

The baby is my daughter, Tami Saj, born in 1974. She continues to live a remarkable life. At age 12 she won medals at her first international swim competition, representing Canada. At age 22 she was inducted into the Northwestern Ontario Sports Hall of Fame after winning over 60 medals for Canada in international swim events, including two Paralympic Games (Seoul and Barcelona). She was the 11th female athlete inducted and the 2nd with a physical disability. An Honors Bachelor of Arts (political studies) graduate of the University of Victoria, she lives in a waterfront condo in Victoria, drives her own car, and works at Royal Roads University. She now plays wheelchair tennis and is a competitive paddler who races with an outrigger canoe club.

Traveling In America

by Mark Kearney

April is the coolest month to head to the heartland of America.

Usually around Easter my wife and I set our sights across the border for a taste of our southern neighbor's life and to soak in the culture and calamity that seems to roil throughout the U.S. of A. Each time, I conjure up the ghost of Kerouac's *On the Road*, read long ago in my undergrad years, and still sticking with me whenever I get behind the wheel of a fully-gassed car on a beckoning highway.

This one particular time we chase the spring season along the spine of the Midwest, the I-75, our destination north Georgia, where we're attending a band camp for adults. We look forward to meeting woodwind and brass players from across North America to blow some Swing and Dixieland.

America, our sometimes-crazy cousin, posts signs at McDonald's entrances warning us not to bring in concealed firearms. It is the land of oversized billboards peeking over treetops to alert us to hotels, restaurants, and a host of services we didn't know we needed, my favorite being the 1-800 number you call for a vasectomy reversal.

We breeze with ease through Michigan and hit Ohio, the Buckeye State; to me, it's more the home of roadkill. Along the highway I count a half dozen dead deer, several groundhogs, and a scattering of stiff skunks and squirrels. The speed limit seems to shift from 55 to 65 depending on, well, it's never really clear, but with the prairie-like landscape we make good time.

The hills begin to roll at Kentucky and the signs of spring are everywhere – greener grass, blooming forsythia, new leaves on the trees. We pass by London, Kentucky, (namesake of our home city in Ontario), snap a quick photo, and hit the obligatory outlet mall. To the sounds of Alanis Morissette and Gordon Lightfoot being piped in (we left Canada hours ago), we find bargains in the clothing stores. Damn the exchange, it's still cheap.

We stop the night at Lexington, discovering virtually all the motels booked because it's the start of horse racing season. We suck back American beer at a chain restaurant and watch a Leave it to Beaver rerun back at the motel on the TV Land channel, America sometimes rubs me the wrong way, but for ungrasped reasons this trip is eminently agreeable.

The next day we slide into the mountainscape of Tennessee, abandoning the golden oldies stations on the car radio to scan for country or bluegrass. We crave southern authenticity and get it from a station spinning gospel tunes and reminding listeners that it's here you can *tune your way to glory*. We tolerate a few songs about the Lord, but being firm walkers along the agnostic/atheist line, we soon shift to a mainstream country station. We decide that someday we should write country songs about middle class angst – *I'm Stuck in the Lineup of the A & P* or *My Lexus Won't Start in the Winter*–titles I file away for the future.

We pull into a rest area for a short break and come across a beautiful stray dog no one seems to know anything about, We curse our lack of a cellphone (one of the few times ever) and worry about the stray for the next 50 miles. By then we've dropped into the west part of North Carolina, careening down a highway so fast I barely notice the sign for Mountainside Chainsaw Art.

In Georgia, the accents are broader, the fruit trees more bounteous; we pull into band camp and for the next four days, I play more clarinet than I normally would in a month. My lip is sagging, but the band is more than 100 strong so I'm just a small blip in the overall sound. We do a killer version of Gershwin's Porgy and Bess medley, and during my few bars of rest I listen to how terrific we sound. Playing this is the highlight–Gershwin's music so quintessentially American.

When we're not playing, we graze on grits, okra, and turnip greens; I want to shout that grits are only palatable with a drip of maple syrup, but I stay silent.

One day we notice one of the car tires is soft, so we drive into town for a solution. Travis, the mechanic, checks it and the other three tires, finds nothing wrong, and refuses payment. *I didn't do much; y'all have a good day,* he drawls, sending us on our way convinced of southern hospitality.

Once band camp is over we point northward, retracing our route to a soundtrack from roots station WDVX in Knoxville. Back in Ohio, we discover, amazingly, that the best place to buy liquor is at the local drug store. Stocked with gin and vodka, we push for Canada.

We hit Ontario on a Saturday morning, eager to be home but still reveling in things American. The official asks us a few questions and then says *welcome back,* the first time I recall ever hearing that from someone at Customs.

I say *thanks,* and the smile stays on my face long after the border has disappeared from our rearview mirror.

##

This story was first published in the London Free Press

Josefina

by Barbara Bunce Desmeules Massobrio

About fifteen years ago, I decided to take Spanish lessons. I had traveled to Honduras the previous year and felt awful at not being unable to communicate. So I enrolled at the local YMCA.

By the end of session two, I felt I needed more practice. I went on the internet and searched pen pal lists in the hope of finding someone with whom to correspond. Most were teens. I kept looking and found Josefina, a middle-aged lady in Guadalajara, Mexico. I sent the first email, she replied and we kept it up.

As my Spanish improved, our friendship grew. We had similar families and similar interests. We talked about our lives and loves. She inspired me with her logic, her kindness and her humanity. We became close friends, without ever exchanging a picture or talking. This became a real relationship on a virtual network in the real world.

A few years later, in 1999, I told Josefina I was going on a short vacation to Puerto Vallarta, Mexico, with my son. She said that it was only a few hours' drive from her home and that she would come to meet me. She decided to bring her son, Jurgen.

We set up a place and time to meet and I waited anxiously for that day. My son, who is a specialist in internet security, was sure that this was some teenage prankster, impersonating a woman. But I knew that Josefina was real. The evening arrived, we took a taxi to the restaurant, and finally we met. Yes, she was a real person. We talked and talked, glad not to have to figure out my spelling in Spanish.

The next day, we left the boys on the beach and she took me driving around the area. We couldn't get enough of each other's company. She was exactly the person she projected in her letters. It was wonderful to be with the real woman behind the letters.

The holidays ended. Home and work were waiting for me back in Montreal. We parted and promised to keep writing.

In August of 2001, my husband and I separated after a 34 year marriage. I was devastated. I wrote to Josefina and asked if I could come to Guadalajara. *Something terrible has happened to me.*

No questions asked; she said yes. I bought a ticket and left. I boarded the plane, held back tears all the way to Guadalajara. When I arrived she put her arms around me and I let it all go. I couldn't speak. I sobbed. I tried to talk but my Spanish was suffering, too.

During the week that I was there, she kept me busy. She said that I would not have time to weep. So, she swept me and my pain throughout the surrounding countryside. She laughed at my fear of the unruly Mexican drivers. She suggested that I take the wheel for a while to get used to it but I refused. *I can't think like Mexican drivers,* I said.

When I left to go back home, I was refreshed and repaired. This wonderful angel had taken care of me, with love, understanding and tenderness.

We continued to correspond. One day she wrote that times were tough in Mexico. The economy was bad. She had lost most of her clients in the small business she ran and had to find other work.

She no longer could afford the internet at home so she would go to an internet cafe. Her letters were short. The emails were further and further apart, until, one day, I realized that I had not heard from her in a long while. I sent email after email and each was returned *address unknown.* I tried calling but the phone was disconnected. I searched for her on the internet. I found a lady with the same name, wrote her a note but it was not my Josefina.

I became obsessed. I searched and left messages on all kinds of sites and groups. I searched her sons' names and never came up with a link. I sent a letter to her home address, explaining how I was looking for my lost friend. I thought that if she had moved, the new owners might know where she was. I never received a reply. I searched for almost two years.

This fall an old high school friend of mine was moving from British Columbia to retire near Guadalajara. I told her the story. She searched the internet in Mexico and found Jurgen's name, the company he worked for and a telephone number. A Mexican friend called and was told that he had changed jobs. The next afternoon, I thought I would try the number myself.

I found him. I couldn't believe that I was in contact. He remembered me. However, he had sad news. Josefina had died in an automobile accident almost two years ago.

Somehow, I had known it would be something terrible. She never would have terminated our friendship like that. I thought that if it was something fixable, I would go and help her as she had helped me. It wasn't.

Jurgen wrote me a beautiful note:

> Hello Barbara,
>
> I feel bad that I had to give you the bad news about my mother.
>
> What I can tell you is that my mother always talked about you and how happy she was to have you as a friend. She always wanted to go to Montreal to visit you. I can tell you that because I am very bad

remembering names but when you said you were calling from Canada, your name instantly came to my mind.

I wish you the best and whenever you want, feel free to contact me.

All the best,

Jurgen

I have lost Josefina but I'm heartened that it wasn't our friendship that died.

##

Before Columbo

by Barbara Florio-Graham

He's ageless, that bumbling detective in the rumpled raincoat. Since his first appearance in 1971 as Columbo, Peter Falk has delighted television audiences around the world, in an astounding 65 productions.

So it's hard to believe that the ordinary guy who just happened to also be a brilliant detective turns 84 this year.

Falk claims he'll never retire. A new movie, ironically titled *Retirement,* was made a few years ago, and he has several other projects in the works, perhaps even another Columbo movie.

Like many fans, I love to watch Columbo, amazed that Falk always remains the same, even though co-stars, settings, and locations change over the years.

But I remember him most clearly in an athletic supporter.

His masculinity is discreetly covered by tights, of course, because my memory of Peter Falk dates from before the let-it-all-hang-out 60s.

It was 1955, and I was a student at Barnard College, part of Columbia University in New York City. As a member of the

Drama Workshop, I had been appointed stage manager for our current theatrical offering.

Workshop Director Norris Houghton divided his time between producing plays at the off-Broadway Phoenix Theatre and teaching drama at Barnard.

After we had decided to attempt Thomas Middleton's *The Changeling*, we ran into a casting problem. We had been unable to find a student actor to play the crucial role of DeFlores.

Would we be willing, Houghton proposed, to consider a young actor he'd just auditioned for the Phoenix? At 29, he was just a few years older than most of us, and had decided to leave his business career for acting. Houghton felt certain he would take part in our amateur production to gain experience playing the villain in a Jacobean melodrama.

Falk was treated just like the rest of us. The newspaper photo accompanying an article on the play did not even identify him by name.

One of Houghton's clever ideas for portraying the duality of DeFlores' personality was to give Peter a disfiguring, port-wine birthmark on the left side of his face. His initial entrance was on the floor level, where a single spotlight picked up the handsome profile as he crossed in front of the stage and mounted the steps onto the platform.

Then, with a flourish of his black cape, he turned to the audience, revealing the grossly deformed left side of his face for the first time. The audience reacted with a collective gasp.

None of us at that time realized then that Peter had only one eye. He had lost the other one to cancer at age three, and it gave him an odd squint which caused that eyelid to droop a bit. It actually gave his handsome face more character.

He was easy to work with, asking for no special consideration from our student group, until production week.

By then, I was overwhelmed with the mechanics of running the backstage apparatus, juggling light and sound cues, directing the stage crew, and even pulling the curtain by hand.

Peter came to me in his costume, announcing that he would need an athletic supporter. *Fine,* I replied. *Buy whatever you need and we'll reimburse you.*

You're the stage manager, right? he answered, in the gruff voice we all came to know years later as Lt. Columbo. *You buy it.*

I was too intimidated to argue. This was the uptight 50s, an era when sanitary products were kept discreetly behind the counter, and there were no ads for men's bikini underwear.

I had grown up in a second-generation Italian household, with two sisters but no brothers. I wasn't sure what an athletic supporter looked like, and had only a vague idea of what it was for.

I went to the campus pharmacy, to the gentle, elderly man from whom I bought *unmentionables*, in a whisper, when the store was almost empty. I explained that I was stage-managing a play whose male characters were attired in doublet and hose, and he, bless him, understood immediately.

What size? he asked. Panic colored my cheeks.

Why don't you take a medium, he suggested, when I didn't answer. I grabbed the package, paid him, and rushed out the door.

I left the parcel in Peter's dressing room.

Five days later, *The Changeling* curtain went up, on time. I didn't forget any cues, nothing fell over as we changed the sets, nobody forgot their lines, and Norris Houghton told us he was proud of our accomplishment.

Soon after, Peter Falk was cast as the bartender in the acclaimed Phoenix production of O'Neill's *The Iceman Cometh*, and went on to Hollywood for his first movie role.

Over the past half century he has appeared in more than 50 films, been nominated for two Oscars, created more than 75 Columbo and other movies for TV, has won several Emmys, and has starred on Broadway. He was the first actor to be nominated for an Oscar and an Emmy in the same year, and the *old* Columbo (which lasted seven seasons) has been shown around the world.

In 1989, when he was 62, Falk revived Columbo, becoming Executive Producer. He began to write and direct new episodes, earning another generation of admirers.

We all long for him to don the crumpled trenchcoat one more time, point that cigar, and say, *Just one more thing*.

But every time I see Peter Falk on TV, I think about *The Changeling* and the athletic supporter.

I never did find out if it fit.

This story was first published in EMMY Magazine

What In The World

Rolling Stones: A Bang For All Generations

by Trudy Kelly Forsythe

HAMPTON: It's 10:30 a.m. on Saturday, Sept. 3. The kids are off to Grandma's house for a sleepover. The sun is shining. It's a perfect day for an outdoor concert.

My husband, Dana, and I, along with two thirty-something friends, get into our van and head towards Moncton for the Rolling Stones' Bigger Bang tour. With over 80,000 fans expected to congregate on the Magnetic Hill concert site, it is the largest scheduled stop for the Stones' yearlong tour.

SUSSEX: It's 10:30 a.m. on Saturday, Sept. 3. The sun is shining. It's a perfect day for an outdoor concert. Nadine Mazerolle, 20, hops into a car with three twenty-something friends.

We've all heard traffic will be crazy and the usual hour-long drive is expected to take between two and three hours.

MONCTON: We can't believe our luck when we arrive before noon at my parents' home on Indian Mountain Road, just two country roads away from the concert site. We have lunch and a few drinks then around 3:00, the four of us hop into my father's truck (it's like being a teenager again) and he drops us about three kilometres from the site. As we walk, I wonder at the range of ages.

Mazerolle and her friends arrive and park in one of the fields being used for parking. They hang out for a half hour then walk about two kilometres to the concert site.

When we heard the Stones were coming to Moncton we knew we had to go. When would we ever get a chance to see the Rolling Stones in our own backyard again? But my age was starting to show. I became concerned about the weather, the crowds, what I could take in (sneaking in a disposable camera was a must; I'm not THAT old!) and, of course, the bathroom facilities.

The concern about bathroom facilities four months before the event told me I had officially entered the next generation. In the former generation, concert-going planning was simple: Gather as many people as you could, buy your tickets and head to the concert. The biggest concern was finding the spot that offered the best vantage point to (a) watch the bands and (b) get to the beer servers quickly.

This event would attract tens of thousands of people to a large field without toilet facilities; imagine my surprise that my main concern was just that, the toilet facilities. I have been to outdoor concerts before with large numbers of people. I saw Bryan Adams, Sloan and Sass Jordan when they performed at Shediac's Parlee Beach in 1992. Friends and I drove to Halifax to see Great Big Sea on Citadel Hill in 1998. More importantly, I recall the state of the porta-potties at both events. Not a pretty sight.

I knew if the New Brunswick Department of Public Health said public events like this mother-of-all-outdoor concerts required one portable toilet for every 100 non-beer drinking or 50 beer-drinking people in attendance then there were going to be well over 1,000 porta-potties on site. My question: How would I know only 50 people had used that toilet, especially after standing in line with over 50 people? How would I find the one that wasn't so bad in the Land of Potty?

Answer? It wasn't going to happen. So I planned ways to make sure Nature did not call. That meant no beer drinking. I actually wondered how little water I could drink to avoid dehydration, but not have to make a visit to Porta-Potty Town. But on the off chance Nature did call, I planned to take a roll of toilet paper, and my cell phone just in case I got lost in the porta-potty village.

On Sept. 3 fans of all ages headed to Magnetic Hill to see 62-year-old Mick Jagger strut his stuff. From the opening fireworks leading into *Start Me Up* to the closing display following the single encore performance of *Satisfaction*, it was amazing, no matter what generation you were from.

Mazerolle and her friends arrived at the concert site soon after it opened at noon; they managed to work their way through the crowd to be in the front row when the Stones ran on stage.

When the French band, Les Trois Accords, started, we decided to make our way down, said Mazerolle, explaining they took it in stages and really strategized to get to the front. *We started by making a lot of noise and dancing to get people to move out of our way.*

When Our Lady Peace took to the stage, Mazerolle and her group were still pretty far back, so they made a train and plowed through. As Maroon 5 finished its set, they were just 10 rows back from the stage.

They pushed their way to the third row. Because it was so crowded, security kept pulling out people. By the time the Tragically Hip finished their performance, they were at the coveted front row.

It was incredibly squishy, said Mazerolle. *It was horrible.* She held onto the railing until the Stones took to the stage shortly before 8:30 p.m., and is glad she did.

Keith Richards was strumming his guitar right in front of us most of the show, said Mazerolle. *We saw everything, right up to every wrinkle.*

My group of thirty-somethings had no intention of heading toward the front. We found a spot in one of the beer gardens, towards the top of the hill, with a great view of the stage and video screens and a fair bit of space between people.

As Mazerolle and her friends strategized their way to the front, we hooked up with other friends, sat on sweaters between bands, and simply enjoyed the fabulous weather, the cool refreshments and the festive atmosphere.

After talking with Mazerolle about her Big Bang experience, I realized the generation gap wasn't so wide. We all worried about the traffic in and out of the show. We all wanted the weather to be nice. We both snuck in disposable cameras. And while this thirty-something crew stayed towards the back of the crowd, others worked their way down as near as they could.

I'm not sure how many in the under-25 crowd took extra toilet paper or thought about the state of the porta-potties, but no matter what age, we'll all remember the day we partied with the Rolling Stones on Magnetic Hill with over 80,000 of our closest friends.

##

Portions of this story were first published in the Kings County Record

Rocks

by Barbara Florio-Graham

Although Air Canada attached *Heavy Baggage* tags to our luggage when we returned from three weeks in the west, the cab driver groaned as he lifted our suitcases into his trunk. *What've you got in here, lady,* he asked, *rocks?*

I hate to lie, so I ignored his question.

And who could possibly understand why I'd gathered golden layers of shale from the Icefield Parkway, lumps of basalt from Bridal Veil Falls, or deep red sandstone from Jasper?

While other visitors to Calgary were buying items bearing the logo of the 88 Olympics, I spent $2 on raw slabs of jade and $3 on a gypsum rose. Other women talked their husbands into stopping at the jewelry store; mine learned long ago that my favorite place to shop is a natural history or science museum.

Several times, he parked beside the road and waited patiently for me to retrieve a sample of aggregate shot with shiny mica, or to fill my pockets with tiny pebbles of creamy calcite.

How did all this begin? My mother admits she might be at fault, for indulging me when I returned from the beach one summer with a canvas bag full of stones.

I was eight or nine, and she assumed, having seen my two older sisters safely through pre-adolescence, that I'd outgrow the collecting habit as they did.

When the assorted rocks adorned my high school bedroom and then followed me to university, both she and my sisters tried to divert my interest into more suitable collections. I maintain, to this day, an assortment of butterfly pins and racks of souvenir coffee spoons, but I haven't given up my rocks.

Collecting objects that are either *useful* or have some intrinsic value has always been condoned by society. If you amass cabinets full of figurines, china plates, stamps, coins or rare books, there is an assumption that these items will increase in value and are therefore a good investment. Similarly, as long as my butterfly pins can be worn as jewelry or my coffee spoons used by visitors when we entertain, they are acceptable.

Even the many shells I've accumulated from years of living on the ocean can be put to use. Small shells can be made into jewelry, while larger ones can hold plants or candles, or used for ashtrays, soap dishes, or paper clip containers.

But what can you do with rocks? A few of the largest specimens make unwieldy doorstops, but just how many paperweights do you think one household can use?

Some, of course, are attractive conversation pieces: the nuggets of raw amethyst and shiny cubes of pyrite, the sparkling quartz cavern inside the geode—these are logical adornments for a coffee table.

But the antique blue glass bowl filled with lace agates in several colors and tumbled pebbles whose origins I have long forgotten? Or the shards of slate, piece of petrified wood, obsidian arrowhead, and lumps of volcanic lava which sit among the silver vases and crystal bowls in my dining room?

My former husband made concessions to my eccentricity. When we cut down a huge poplar tree in the back yard and didn't know what do with the stump, he agreed to cover it with earth and black plastic to create a rock garden.

Indoors, he reinforced the living room bay window so that the plants that thrive there can sit on humidity trays filled with interesting stones.

But it does get embarrassing. I still blush when visitors ask about the geode.

It was many years ago, when my parents joined a motorhome caravan to Mexico. When one of the other men suggested a side trip to go rock-hounding, my father immediately thought of my collection and agreed.

Pick in hand, guided by his friend, he unearthed a cracked geode, a large, irregular blob of copper aggregate, and some lovely agate slabs in shades from mustard to chocolate.

The first stop on their return was at my older sister's, where their youngest grandchild, David, who was then about twelve, noticed the rocks and asked if he could have them.

Daddy was aghast. *Oh no!* he said, *those are for Bobbi.*

David is married with two daughters now, and has probably forgotten all about the rocks from Mexico. My parents welcomed several great-grandchildren, whose collections include coins, stickers, and teddy bears. We don't intend to tell them that there's a strange aunt in the family who collects rocks.

Unless, of course, one of them makes the mistake of asking for the special piece of topaz quartz my dad got from a friend. He traded, he tells me, two almost- new bicycle tires for it.

I put it beside that mottled grey rock I picked up in Dinosaur Park at the Calgary Zoo. My husband had insisted it was just concrete, made to look vious pagelike prehistoric lava, but I brought it home anyway.

It was in the grey suitcase, I think, the one that had to have the handle repaired.

Again.

This story was first published in the Ottawa Citizen

Pies And Fall Fairs

by Mark Kearney

I haven't listed award-winning piemaker on my résumé just yet, but I could.

Among my several hobbies, I've dabbled in the culinary arts and have some ribbons and a few dollars in prize money to show for it. Call me a Professional Baker.

I know I'll never make it at the Cordon Bleu school or be dishing out pastries to the haute cuisine set. But at the annual Ilderton, Ontario, Fall Fair and even the much larger Western Fair in London, Ontario, my pumpkin pies have scored with the judges. I've never captured the elusive first-place red ribbon, but I've got a second, a few thirds, and a couple of fourths for my efforts. Total prize money–maybe $20.

Admittedly, a good number of those ribbons have come from the quaint and slightly politically incorrect *Anything Baked by a Man* category, but I always proudly point out that I also enter the pumpkin pie events, too, when I can. Western Fair doesn't have a specific pumpkin pie category– shame on them–but Ilderton does, and there I'm up against the best bakers in Middlesex County. It's in that category that I managed the brilliant blue second-place ribbon.

My secret? Brandy. A good dose of brandy does wonders for a pumpkin pie.

This whole competitive bake off has also introduced a new phrase into my vocabulary: *to ribbon*. As a writer I'm not fond of turning nouns into verbs, but if athletes can *medal* at the Olympics I figure I can *ribbon* at fall fairs.

Of course, ribboning isn't my only reason for baking pies. The whole fall fair atmosphere is what makes entering special. I know it's a cliché to say *I'm just happy to participate and if I get a ribbon, well shucks, that's just a bonus.* But I can say that because there have been years when, aw shucks, I didn't get a %$&*## ribbon.

Nevertheless, strolling around the fairs, checking out the other bakers' wares, seeing who grew the largest zucchini, or who came up with the best flower arrangement, are anachronistic delights that we've managed to hang onto in our rush toward modernism. That people are still out there home cooking or decorating in the hopes of winning a ribbon is comforting.

Fall fairs have been with us, in Ontario at least, for more than 200 years. My first ribbons came at the Markham Fall Fair in the early 1960s, when I won prizes for bike decorating and penmanship. I suppose it's long enough ago now that I can come clean on the bike decorating and admit my mother did most (okay, all) of the work on that. But you can't fake great penmanship.

To go to a fall fair these days is to walk back into those golden years when I was a wide-eyed six or seven year old amazed by the variety of displays, carnival rides, farm animals, and dazzling new products that could slice vegetables or shine a car. Or both! They're still with us today, and I'm glad.

So maybe that's why I don't hesitate to enter the *Anything Baked by a Man* category. Its very existence says *we're holding onto things no matter how dated they are.* And I can tell you from experience that it's a tough category. I came third one year at Western Fair to a guy from Bundaberg, Australia. Ever since learning about the competition on the internet, he's apparently sent his fruitcake to London by air express each year, and officials pick it up at customs.

So, I'm not just battling other men in the region; I'm taking on the world.

And please don't assume that this category wouldn't be found at more sophisticated competitions. Last time I checked the Canadian National Exhibition, they had a *Baked by a Man* section, too.

So, like any good professional, who has won his share of prizes, I'm always looking to push myself, find tougher competition, and stretch my baking muscles. I had some success at Ilderton and decided to try the Western Fair. But now that I've won a couple of ribbons from it, I wonder where I should compete next.

The CNE? Maybe the Royal Winter Fair? Or perhaps I should check out a State fair in Michigan or New York.

Nahhh. I'm thinking Bundaberg.

##

This story was first published in The Globe and Mail

Today I Let Go Of The Wall

by Julie V. Watson

Today I let go of the wall!

I was so excited I almost yelled at the top of my lungs. I even phoned my son in Vancouver to crow about my achievement. I'm sure you're wondering about the significance of such a mundane occurrence so let me paint the picture.

Here I was, a 5'1" sixty-something who fears deep water, in a pool that is six feet deep. I felt comfortable enough to let go of the edge of the pool and set off to glide through the water, using a movement like cross-country skiing that makes me feel graceful and energized.

It was a memorable moment. Freeing. I felt flippin' wonderful.

In fact, this sore and aching body of mine suddenly longed to move, to exercise. As a person who hurt from arthritis, needed a double knee replacement, and never liked anything even remotely athletic because I always felt like an uncoordinated klutz, I looked on this as a bit of a miracle.

So what brought me to that memorable time? I had voiced a desire to try aquafit classes for years, but in my usual procrastinating way never acted on it. It took my friend Debbie to get me out of my office and off to the pool.

Several times each week individuals ranging from fragile seniors, to overweight folks, to those with limited mobility (some even in wheelchairs), along with a few svelte young things, do themselves a favor by heading to the pool for exercise and socializing. Aquafit actually encompasses several programs: Aqua Arthritis (easy enough for anyone), Cardio Craze (more high energy), Aqua Jogging, and others, depending on the facility.

We aquafitters are divided. Some who don't like deep water spend the 45-minute class in the leisure pool, which has barrier free access to warm water that is waist to chin deep. Participants don't float, but the water does its job by making for a low-impact workout.

The majority can be found bobbing in the competition pool. Most wear a belt to help them float in an upright position in order to best benefit from the exercise routine. Since intrepid Debbie headed straight into the competition pool I followed along behind.....until I read the depth of the pool. Six feet! All five feet of me screeched to a halt. No way. I need to touch bottom—or at least know I can. The whole head must be above water!

When staff placed portable stairs into the pool, provided all sizes of floatation belts to keep one's head above water, and no one pressured me to *go for the deep side,* I decided to try it. I felt secure in the belt, so cross-handed along the edge to the pool wall and followed the instructor as best I could, albeit with a death grip hold and never venturing more than a few feet from the stairs.

Knowing that no one can see what I'm doing is a huge factor for me. Being naturally uncoordinated and clumsy had always embarrassed me. Not here. The only thing anyone can see is my head bobbing up and down in the water. Cool.

Second class I let go of the wall. Just for a minute, but just a few weeks later I happily moved away to give newcomers the security of the wall to hold onto. Best of all I couldn't wait for aquafit class. Me, looking forward to exercise.

Instructor Marlene leads us through 45 minutes of movement that matters. An arthritis trainer who specializes in water fitness, she knows her stuff. A three-time cancer survivor, she inspires everyone to work for their own health.

As Marlene tells us, there are rules. As she struts between the two pools demonstrating what she wants us to do in the water, she imparts an enthusiasm for moving and respect for those who do what they can. *Listen to your body*, she stresses. *And don't pee in the pool.* Although we all laugh at her levity, none of us would dare!

My own advice: Go on out and try it. Go to a pool where you feel comfortable. Wear a flotation device at least to begin. Once in the water, keep moving. The important thing is to do what you can, as you can, and enjoy. Each day it will be a little more and soon you too will let go of the wall.

This story was first published in The Guardian

Neighborhood Shakeup

by Luigi Benetton

There's nothing like a good action movie to take my mind off my troubles. I used to like walking to the local theater, but since the Humber shut down, that luxury is gone.

So, instead of a film, I caught a free live show Monday night at Runnymede Collegiate. It was about, of all things, the future of the old Humber Theater. Upwards of 100 people came out.

First, we sat through the trailer for the building that will replace the theater. We politely heard the architect PowerPoint his way through the latest design: a ten-story mixed-use retail-condo development, heavy on the condos.

Improvements over the previous design and other selling points came out at every step. Ten stories, not thirteen; 100 feet high, not 130; 50 units, not 92; an award-winning architect came up with the design; it will be a *lantern* (?) at the west end of Bloor Street; the site is underused; it's close to a subway stop and it's on Bloor, so intensification here is good.

When the trailer came to *The End,* the action/horror flick started.

People told tales of conflict in the streets:

You can't turn left from Riverview Gardens (just west of the theater) onto Bloor, so people race through the neighborhood instead.

What will the traffic be like two or three years from now?

I want my street shut down so not just anybody can drive down my street!

They took the fight to the alley:

The laneway behind the building narrows to about ten feet.

Delivery trucks often stop in the laneway to load or unload for other businesses there. (Hopefully not where it narrows to ten feet.)

Part of the laneway belongs to the parking authority. (If the residents can't use it, the building needs an entrance off Bloor Street. Shudder.)

It spilled out into the parking lot:

Where do health club members park?

Are there enough parking spots for residents in the building?

We already have too much permit parking from people who don't live on my street.

To the rooftops:

*Most other buildings on Bloor West are two or three
stories.*

It could get ugly:

We do not have to become Yonge and Eglinton.

It's Bauhaus, Berlin-style.

*As an award-winning architect, do you think you'll be
hanging any awards on your wall for this one?* (The
building fits in with its neighbors. And that's the
problem–the neighboring buildings are ugly.)

Mysterious characters loom on the horizon:

*My kids play in the back yard. Who's looking down on
them?*

It gets intense:

*Just because the site can be intensified doesn't mean it
should be.*

*Do we get a density bonus request if this building goes
through?*

Will it be a life-and-death matter?

(In winter,) *I won't get any sun in my building.*

My poor roses will die! (in this building's shadow).

People want to change the ending:

Make it shorter–take out the health club.

Build stores and the health club, and stop there!

So far, it doesn't look like a box-office smash. Stay tuned for the next installment in the saga of the old Humber Theater.

##

This story was first published in the Bloor West Villager

Back In My Future

by Fred Desjardins

The only thing fast about old age is how quickly it happens.

A couple of months ago I was the proverbial carefree grasshopper blithely turning cartwheels while my friends methodically burrowed away in grim anticipation of the cruelties of winter. Then came the pain. At first it was the periodically familiar shocking volts of excruciata that lanced my lower back as I jumped up from bed in the morning. I put it down to a lifetime of sports abuse. But then came the crippling spasms throughout my upper back and rib cage and the weird sensation that my heart was about to explode.

Fearing the worst, I checked into the emergency ward where the staff went straight to the two likeliest culprits, the heart and lungs. Four hours of poking, prodding, and X-rays later they pronounced that my heart was strong and my lungs as pretty as Bambi's mother before the pyromaniac came to town. The problem was that the symptoms kept getting worse. And so I went to my GP who ordered me to get a more thorough exam.

Results in hand, my doctor sat me down and told me that he had good news and bad. I went for the good news first, which was that there was nothing wrong with my heart, lungs, or vital organs, which meant that The Choir Invisible would be short one baritone for the foreseeable future. The bad news was that I have spinal arthritis, requiring pricey meds, pricier physiotherapy and even pricier health center fees. Oh, and I have to lose 40 pounds in a hurry.

As Einstein said, *All Things Are Relative.* I had expected the doc to tell me either that my jam tart was kaput or that I was riddled with The Big C. Imagine my relief when he gave me a straight A on both counts. Upon leaving his office I was tempted to do a back flip but I settled for a bowl of chicken soup instead. No need to go crazy just because the Governor stayed my execution at the eleventh hour.

Frankly, I see my diagnosis as a much needed kick in the pants as I've let my girlish figure go to seed through bad eating habits and lack of exercise. I have a full-length mirror on my bedroom door that's completely covered in black electrical tape except for the eyes....and even THEY look fat. Now I have a compelling reason to whip myself into shape.

I had a delightful encounter this morning at the fitness center. I called last night and told the bubbly receptionist that I'd come by this morning to sign up. Well, what a fox! A painfully lovely young thing with blue hair and laugh lines deep enough to store olive pits. The vixen must have been in her early 50s but didn't look a day older than 46. In any case, this lust of my life purred that a year's membership would be somewhere in the vicinity of seven million dollars. But God love her, she noted that the senior's discount would cut the price in half. So I quickly forked over my Visa and signed my John Henry.

As I stood up to leave I leaned over the counter and asked her if locks were provided to protect our clothes and valuables. *Of course*, she said. *We're as secure as a church. You can even leave your dentures in your locker. I know I always do.*

And with that I fairly floated to my car, drunk on her perfume, which I recognized as *Evening In Flatbush.*

##

This story was first published in Laugh Your Shorts Off by Writers In Residence Edited by Margie Culbertson

Vegetable Grace

by Joanne Carnegie

So who's this Clem I've been hearing so much about?

It was my friend Susan speaking. Her son plays baseball
with my son, so news travels quickly between the two
households. Susan may be a lawyer by profession, but she
has clearly missed her calling. A hundred years ago she
would have been the village matchmaker.

*Your son says you're spending so much time with Clem, he
hardly sees you anymore!*

Her eyes were bright and searching, like my cat's when he
sees a movement in the bushes. I've been a single parent
now for twelve years, a condition my friend considers an
affront to nature. In her lust to see me married off, Susan
forgot about my son's fine sense of humor.

She was toying with her spoon, feigning an interest in
something happening outside the window. *Sooooo... what
does he do for a living, this Clem?*

I was silent, trying to think of a way to break the news.
Susan looked as if she were about to explode from
curiosity. Finally, in a desperate attempt to squeeze the
juicy details out of me, she tried the humorous approach.
With a name like that, I hope he's not running a still in his

basement! Ah, Clem—the love of my life, the unending focus of my attention.

No, he wasn't making hooch on the sly. In fact, *Clem* was a she. Several *she's*: Anna Louise, Nelly Moser, the Comtesse de Bouchaud, Elsa Späth, Gillian Blades...

My son was right: since discovering the world of clematis early this spring, I've been obsessed with the progress of my vines, mooning over them for hours in the back garden, cataloging every new leaf and flower bud. I lose track of time and have to be called in for dinner. It's the new family joke: when he wants me in, my son throws open the back window and runs the electric can opener. It works for the cat, and since I'm as much in the grip of primal forces as he, why not?

I didn't intend to become a hostage to beauty. When I dug up the ground around a utility pole in the back lane last year, my only aim was to satisfy my curiosity. A friend had given me the classic handful of beans—hyacinth beans in this case, *Dolichos lablab*. Maybe I was under the influence of *Jack and the Beanstalk*, or perhaps it was a developmental thing: having successfully reproduced myself, I was ready to move on to mitosis of the vegetable sort.

Every obsession starts from one such small seed, and mine was the sight of a carpet of purple-veined heart-shaped leaves twining their way up the pole, crowned by little mauve flowers that turned into plump, sparrow-shaped magenta pods. One day I found a neighbor I'd had arguments with standing by the pole, smoking reflectively. He looked up at me, and gesturing in the direction of the beans, said with unrestrained admiration, *It's nice, what you do here.*

I was hooked.

Spurred by my success, this year I moved on to clematis. Observing the sacred rites, I buried the root balls deep in the center of rich black loam fortified with magic: compost, bone meal, and a touch of dolomitic lime. With a handful of alfalfa meal, a spoonful of algae and a whisper of greensand, the feast was complete.

Gardening is the most humble and satisfying alchemy, a kind of Zen practice. All it asks of its acolytes is sweat, mindful attention, and patience.

The yield of my labors with clematis has been astonishing, both in floral abundance and in improved relations with my neighbors.

Gardening is a natural ice-breaker. Suddenly, on account of a few vines, people I'd never seen before have emerged out of their cocoons to come talk with me. Those I knew only by sight or exchanged hellos with have lingered long enough to reveal their personalities. People are generous with their appreciation, overlooking the unfinished bits, ignoring the parts that don't quite work yet.

There's a quiet sort of gratitude in those who stop by, as if I've made them a new Eden. I feel more rooted in the neighborhood as a result, and have been encouraged enough to expand my horticultural efforts to the front yard.

Which includes, of course, more clematis. I've tucked a *durandii* along the front wrought-iron fence, where I'm hoping its floral grace will work the same magic as its sisters out back. No doubt it will: who can resist the charms of these floral sirens?

Not Marjorie Harris, the gardening writer par excellence. *Clematis, Queen of the vines,* she says with unalloyed exuberance, *is a magnificent cover-up for all that lies ugly upon the earth.*

And I would add, for all that lies ugly in human relations as well. In the fairy tale, Jack finds gold at the end of his horticultural foray. I have found an even better bounty: the friendship of my neighbors, a benediction bestowed by flowers and greenery. Even Susan is all smiles, despite her initial disappointment.

Clematis, she pointed out with that look on her face again, *would make a dandy wedding bouquet.*

This story was first published in The Globe and Mail

Love And Loss

Funny Man Blues

by Fred Desjardins

I've been a humor writer for a quarter of a century and a humor-writing teacher for nearly that long. I didn't just wake up one day and say, *You know, I'm tired of selling pencils in front of the liquor store. I think I'll become an internationally renowned humorist.* I had been practicing my craft for years, writing rude poems on the public washroom walls of the nation. So it's not like I went into this thing blind.

However, as my comedic star slowly rose I realized I'd have to branch out if I wanted to make enough money to partake of luxuries like food and shelter. My first move was to land a spot teaching humor writing. Still, I wasn't making ends meet and so I began writing features for newspapers and magazines on every topic imaginable, most of which were remarkably uninteresting: Table-tennis tournaments, the menace of grade school littering, the dos and don'ts of firecracker safety, and the inexact science of dandruff prevention, to name a few.

I was finally earning enough to sustain myself but suddenly I found that I was having trouble finishing articles. Smack dab in the middle of a sentence my mind would go blank and all I could think about was the rising cost of Kraft Dinner or the relative advantages of two-ply toilet tissue. I was shaken up and it took a while to discover that I was suffering from a very common malaise known as writer's block.

Talk to any professional writer and they'll all tell you that the biggest problem they face is the dreaded writer's block. It doesn't matter whether they're writing about civil rights, the heartbreak of psoriasis, or Winston Churchill's frightening love of nudism. At some point, writers hit an invisible wall that prevents them from completing their work. The suggested solutions for this malady run the gamut from jogging backwards to Jakarta to taking a freezing cold shower in combat fatigues holding a parasol to protect the twelve-inch cigar clenched between their teeth. Most suggested strategies fall somewhere in between because Indonesia can only be accessed by thousands of miles of ocean and most Westerners have sworn off smoking.

My advice to fellow writers experiencing such mindlock is to engage in what I call *freestyle writing*. When I'm stuck in the middle of trying to wax eloquent about the crucial importation of buck-toothed hogs from Transylvania I find salvation in tossing off crazed diatribes to my peers. Many of these missives look like this:

News Flash: 700 Mexicans attempting to illegally enter California were detained today by the border police. Rather than send them back to Tijuana, American officials have decided to send a stern warning to other potential illegal aliens by sending the group to a much more forbidding place: Atlantic City. New

Jersey officials were unavailable for comment as they were either clinging to life from blunt instrument trauma or betting their internal organs on a fixed dice game.

Admittedly, my strategy doesn't work for every writer but it's freed me to complete whatever stunningly uninteresting article I must finish in order to pay the bills. Welcome to the truth behind the fabled romance of the writer. That's not to say that it's not possible to live the dream: J.K. Rowling holds the holy grail that we all aspire to. So yes, you can get there from here but it's a longshot at best. Unless you enjoy churning out copy extolling the virtues of the potato trade with Ireland.

However, there is a writer's block that I can never surmount. A topic so painful that it confounds all strategies:

She was christened *Mary* in the Spring of 1959 but that moniker never stuck as my mother tagged her *my little cookie.* Cookie she became, except for meaningless birth certificates, driver's licenses, and pathologically correct Catholic School teachers. She was a strange child to me and my other sister, Denise. Cookie looked like an Eskimo, and unlike us, she was completely without guile or self interest, skills we honed as hard-bitten ghetto kids. If we all had the same amount of red licorice, Denise and I would eat ours quickly, knowing that Cookie would give us her last pieces.

Mom worked two jobs to keep us from starving to death in our cold water flat with the slanted floors and the dank smell of poverty and despair. And so Denise and I became Cookie's Mom and Dad. We washed her, dressed her, fed her, and put her to bed at a decent hour. I was ten, Denise was six, and Cookie was three. No time for childhood. We had a job to do.

That job ended May 30, 1995. I took the call from a relative in Spokane, Washington, telling me that my baby sister had been murdered by her husband in front of their five young children. She was stabbed 31 times with a butcher knife. Her final words were, *Help me.*

I immediately made plans to travel there, picking up my distraught mother in Vancouver along the way. Before I reached there my mother had been interviewed by the scandal-sheet TV program, *Inside Edition.* That only added sensationalistic humiliation to the grief. They asked me to appear and I told them to f%#$k off.

Three hellish years later, my mother and I traveled to Spokane for the final trial of my sister's killer. The American justice system is quite different from the Canadian system in that judges must stand for election every four years; the presiding female judge was expected to lose her election because she had a reputation of favoring women in court cases. And so her ruling did not come as a complete surprise. She sentenced my sister's husband to five years, with the proviso that he would be freed after two years given *good behavior.* My mother was devastated. As we drove back to Vancouver she barely said a word.

I left her in her one-bedroom apartment shortly thereafter, pressed to come back by my wife and children. A week later I took the call that told me that my mother had taken her life.

It's often been said that the worst thing that can happen in life is for a parent to have their child die. I was Cookie's Dad and Denise was her Mom. When we lost Cookie, Denise moved to Vancouver (the geographical cure) and I stayed in Halifax. We rarely speak to each other anymore and neither of us can tell the world what Cookie meant to us.

Everything that mattered was said in May of 1995. The one writer's block that can never be conquered.

##

My Life Now

by Barbara Bunce Desmeules Massobrio

Tonight will be my first night alone since Giorgio has gone. I am afraid. But, when I lay my head on the pillow that first night, I asked him to help me sleep. I promised not to cry in bed. I felt his hand caress my face as he used to do. I don't want him to leave me. If I didn't have children that I would never willingly hurt, I would try to join him. Instead, I will have to wait.

This morning I woke up feeling that I had slept, at least for a good 6 hours. It felt good. One of my sons had slept over and I went to bed with the door open to the living room where he was watching football. I asked him to leave the light on and door open; it felt more lived in. I fell asleep quickly. Not as many bad dreams. Also, no two layer sleeping: one half of the brain asleep and the other thinking. It was a good night. He said it was for him too, because he has a young baby at home and is awakened several times a night. Well, I don't feel as guilty having him then. It gives him a break. His wife told me it is a break for her, too.

I had an appointment this morning and I was afraid to go outside and see people. All of those happy people going about their day, carefree. I suppose everyone has an invisible pain. Mine shows on my swollen eyes, nose and cheeks. I am an ugly crier. I can't believe the world hasn't stopped.

I can go along for a while and feel okay, well, not sick. But then the pain hits me from behind, like an unexpected wave hits you in the back when you are in the ocean just looking at the beach and dreaming. Smack. It knocks me down. I can't stop it. I just feel that huge hole in my stomach come up into my chest and I cry. I sob. I sob loud and hard and probably scare anyone who hears me. My little grandson came over to me and rubbed my arm yesterday when I broke down. It was the sweetest little touch. Like a little angel.

Tonight, I decided that I would go for a walk. I put on a jacket and running shoes and stepped outside. I was scared to be out there. I felt vulnerable for some reason. Out in the open, my pain perhaps visible to everyone.

As I stepped onto the sidewalk I noticed a lady (a stranger) walking along coming up by where I was. I asked her if she was going for a walk. She said yes. I asked her if she minded if I walked with her. She looked at me oddly and said yes. I told her that my husband had just died. I cried. I told her I wanted to walk but felt alone. She told me that she knew how I felt. Her husband of 25 years had died 15 years ago. Another angel, She modified her route and walked around my neighborhood and we talked. She said that the remembering will always be there and be hard but that life goes on. Time heals. Trite, she said, but true. I asked her if she talked to him. She said yes. I told her I was talking to Giorgio and I was glad to hear I am not alone to do this. She said it helps. She told me to also keep walking every day and that would help. I asked her to excuse me for accosting a total stranger; this is not my style, but she understood. Then, she turned in her direction and I went home.

Now, I remind myself that writing is also a therapy for me. So, I am writing this. This is good enough. As my Giorgio would say: Good enough for mining purposes.

##

Paul

by Hilda Young

PAUL EDWARD HANNA: SEPTEMBER 18 1983 TO OCTOBER 3 2005

Life has not been the same since my son Paul died.

The autopsy came back inconclusive as it was almost five days before he was found and deterioration had set in. The only known fact was that a large amount of the medication he used to treat his bipolar condition was missing. It appeared he took an overdose.

There was no note and no obvious reason. However, from reading through his binder I think he felt overwhelmed after his grandmother died and could not cope with his school work.

I have talked to various professionals about his condition but it has been very frustrating as my ideas about support seem to conflict with the *legal* protectionist aspect of the law. According to Grant Meadwell, head of counseling services at Fleming College, where Paul was enrolled as a student, students must sign a release form in order for the school to share personal information with a third party. Without a release form, school employees are only able to share policies and procedures. In addition, a trip to the counselors can be enforced only if there is a behavior

117

problem. Mr. Meadwell said that Paul's case caused much distress among those who knew him.

However, I still wonder what we could have done to prevent the tragedy. I was in contact with Jonathan Paynter, Paul's counselor, for a few months after he died. I had lots of suggestions but the reality is no one can make anyone talk or request help and Paul did not like to ask for help.

As a family we have all dealt with the reality differently. We still have Paul's files on the main computer memory. We donated his text books to the school when we attended the first awards night after his death.

I took a proactive stand: I contacted the school and sought counseling; I tracked down the more than $1000 donated to Scouts Canada in his memory; the Paul Edward Hanna bursary at Fleming College has grown rapidly with no extra fundraising, just me pushing my connections. I do not know if people are still donating to it. I do not know who received it this school year.

Others became involved: The Environmental Technician Program that Paul was enrolled in created an award in his memory to be given out at June graduation.

I find some comfort in that so much good is being done in memory of Paul. But I ask myself: What can we learn from having a child with bipolar?

Patience. It is a mental illness that can be treated. However, the child has to be watched discreetly to see if there are changes in moods. Any adults or medical people interacting with the child need to be told of the condition. I think the main reason Paul died is that the teachers were not aware of his condition so did not take note when he did not show up for classes after his grandmother died.

If only I knew what triggered that final act!

##

A Tree Of Memories

by Helen Lammers-Helps

You'll never find our Christmas tree featured on the pages of a designer magazine. Our tree isn't decked out in the latest decorating fad. There are no matching pink and white Victorian lace bows. There's no fuchsia and purple frippery, or whatever the latest trend is in Christmas tree decorating. Instead, our tree is a hodgepodge of ornaments collected over the years, but each holds a memory dear to our hearts.

There are the inexpensive wooden ornaments I bought when my husband and I were newly married and money was tight. These are a reminder of simpler times when there were just the two of us.

Later, when each of our children was born, I bought a special ornament engraved with his or her name and date of birth to mark the new addition to the family.

Then there are the little hand-made ornaments the children made at school over the years – construction paper angels and clay Christmas trees. These are a little the worse for wear as it is difficult to pack them away year after year without them getting crushed. Still, each one is special as a reminder of Christmases past and a record of each child's progress from pre-school to middle school.

For several years we were in the habit of purchasing Christmas ornaments as vacation souvenirs. So we have Mickey Mouse and Donald Duck ornaments as reminders of our trip to Disney World hanging alongside little glass ornaments from the Caribbean and little wooden ornaments from a craft shop near the cottage we rented one summer.

Then there are all the angel ornaments given to us in memory of our infant son, Michael, who died just before Christmas. They are made of many different materials— metal, clay, porcelain, wood, glass. Some are simple while others are very elaborate. When we hang them on our tree each year it feels like we've included Michael in our Christmas celebration.

The last ornament we hang on our tree has special significance. This little porcelain angel was given to us by precious friends, on what would have been our son's first birthday, for they knew it would be a difficult time of year for us. I'll always remember the note that was attached to the angel. The note said that they had bought one just like it for themselves and that each year when they hung it on their own Christmas tree, they would think of Michael, too. It meant so much to us: not only did they acknowledge Michael's short life, but they are including him in their own Christmas traditions; this spoke volumes to us at a time when we felt very alone with our grief.

So even though our tree, with its mismatched assortment of ornaments, won't win any designer competitions, we enjoy its simple beauty. Each ornament holds a special place in our hearts, reminding us of the love in our lives, and that's what I want to be reminded of at Christmas time.

##

About Joanna

by Lorri Benedik

My husband looked up from his Saturday Gazette. "Honey, I think your friend's mom passed away." I peeked over his shoulder. There it was. I began reading and then stopped. "They made an unforgivable mistake," I complained. "It says here she was predeceased by her beloved daughter, Joanna—surely they mean survived." Then, my stomach sank, I had been trying, unsuccessfully, to reach my friend for almost two weeks.

The corridor of Concordia University's Hall building, in Montreal, was thick with students searching for assigned classrooms; their chatter was deafening. I caught her eye, flashed a wry smile and said, *You again? Are you sure you're not stalking me?* It was the fourth time, in as many days, that I'd seen her. *My name's Joanna,* she said, pumping my hand firmly.

We sat together in class and soon became friends. Joanna was a great listener. Her dark hair and eyelashes contrasted strikingly with blue-green eyes that twinkled like gemstones. At 28, she was mother to three kids aged eight, six and four. She adored her *babies.*

We began spending school holidays together. My five-year-old son, Zach, and I would drive over and hang out. Joanna showed me that it cost little to keep kids happy.

Once they spent an entire morning caring for an ailing caterpillar the kids named *Stripy*. An old shoebox became his infirmary. They scoured the park for just the right type of leaves for the insect's comfort and nourishment. Joanna's youngest and Zach teamed up. They knew that Stripy needed water and debated, at length, which type of container would be best. They even tried feeding him tiny drops, from a spoon. Soon, he was proclaimed miraculously cured. They bid a tearful farewell to Stripy, patted his furry back and placed him in a shady spot. His destiny was to become an exquisite butterfly.

Another day was spent hitting tennis balls against the wall of a nearby community centre. As a special treat we had lunch at McDonald's. Joanna reminded the children to save their paper cups and lids for our after-lunch activity – grasshopper hunting. In a field of long, straw-like grass we chatted for hours while the kids chased, captured and released dozens of grasshoppers. This was close to heaven, for Zach. That evening, he asked, *Mom, when can we go see my kids again?*

The following year, one of our courses was *Self-Managed Learning*. It challenged each student to design an individual learning project – one that pushed us to acquire new skills, directly affecting our lives.

Joanna created a survey for children that revealed their natural learning styles – a valuable tool for parents and teachers. It was a brilliant piece of work. My friend was destined for greatness.

Then, after the mid-winter holiday, she didn't show up for our *Leadership* course. I called during the break and her husband answered. He said that Joanna had been suffering with severe migraines and had been admitted to hospital for tests – he refused to tell me where. *She doesn't want to see anyone,* he said. I needed to hear it from her.

I assumed my private investigator persona and tracked her down in a psychiatric facility. That day I learned that my friend suffered from bipolar disorder. During her long hospitalization her family told everyone she was *staying with an aunt.* Like many who face mental illness, they felt ashamed and feared social stigma.

Once she was discharged, our friendship resumed seamlessly. Slowly, Joanna reclaimed her sparkle. But one of our conversations frightened me. She said, *My medication makes me groggy. I can't wait to stop taking it.* I said, *Joanna, what I understand is that you have to keep taking the meds so the symptoms don't come back.* She replied, *No, no. I'm sure I can stop when I feel better.* I made her promise that she wouldn't stop without her doctor's consent.

But that's the thing about this cruel disease. When the drugs are working, you feel like you don't need them. And that's what happened to my dear friend. She stopped her meds and slipped into a deep abyss. Joanna then took her own life.

I left my husband's side and quickly dialed her parents' number.

"Hello, Mr. S., it's Lorri speaking, Joanna's friend. I just read about your wife. I'm so sorry for your loss. But they made a terrible error in the paper. It says that Joanna pre-deceased her."

"It's true, Lorri," he said, his voice cracking. "Joanna passed away ten days ago. After that, my wife couldn't bear it—her heart just broke."

This story was first published in the Concordia University alumni magazine

Remembering My Father

by Irene Davis

My dad—my kids' grandfather—died last fall.

His final illness put us all through a five-and-a-half-week meat grinder, as he lay suffering in his hospital bed. When it was over, the memories poured in, as we tried to sort through what he had meant to us.

How do you do that? How do you measure a life, measure the influence it had on you?

Perhaps begin with who he was.

When my father died he had been married 62 years. He was active to the end, physically as much as he was able, mentally to the full extent of his considerable intellect.

He had lived long enough to count among his descendants five grandchildren plus three spouses, and four great grandchildren, the last one born in Australia while he lay in his hospital bed, and in time for him to know about her.

In his lifetime my dad demanded much of himself in terms of achievement. He was a successful businessman who provided his customers with excellence in product and service. Although he had never had the opportunity to go to university, he knew more than many college grads. He read and studied all his life, everything from history to religion to Hebrew to math. Among my childhood memories are pictures of my dad working out complicated calculus problems—this was recreation, mind you.

He expected from his children and grandchildren what he expected of himself: That we love learning, that we achieve something in life, that we strive for excellence. I think that each of us in his or her own way made him happy and proud. I know he loved us all, for what he couldn't say in words he communicated in deeds.

I remember, for example, trips to Niagara Falls during blossom time, along the old Welland Canal road. I remember waiting and watching as the bridge lifted and the boat slowly sailed through. I remember climbing with him the steps of the Brock Monument in Queenston Heights, and my disappointment at the top when instead of a wide and glorious panorama there was only a small opening to peer through.

I remember that when I was stricken with appendicitis at camp he drove all night to bring me back to Toronto from the village hospital. After the surgery he brought me a box of chocolates, although he had been after me to lose weight. He figured the treat was more important. (He was a sucker for sweets like chocolate and quality jam, and my husband and I often brought special jams like ginger or gooseberry back from trips for him.)

I remember also that he taught me to read when I was three years old, and introduced me to Dickens' *Pickwick Papers* when I was 13. My love of books I owe to him, not to a school teaching system that picked apart the words until there was nothing of beauty or interest left. And without his patient teaching of concepts and principles there are physics and math courses I would never have passed. He also taught me not to give up when it got tough, to keep plugging.

I remember that when his grandchildren and great grandchildren were infants he would only look at them, not hold them, for he considered infants to be fragile and breakable, and he was quite sure he would be the one to break them. His time would come when they were older.

Unfortunately, he did not live long enough to build connections with his great grandchildren, although he enjoyed them tremendously when he saw them. The oldest may barely remember him; the others not at all.

His grandchildren, however, do have memories. One remembers that his grandfather gave him his first job, another that he tried to teach him to play chess, but it didn't take, a third that when as a child she inadvertently caught him in an embarrassing position, he subsequently sat down with her and gave her a Hebrew lesson as a way of easing the awkwardness.

When his grandchildren were young he took them each year to Niagara Falls—just him and the kids, the rest of us were not invited. There he gave them the works. They climbed down the gorge, went under the falls, had a wonderful, exhausting time and came home tired, dirty and content.

One year they discovered St. David fudge. At the time there was no store, just a house, with a sign beside one window saying *fudge*. The transaction took place through that window.

One taste, of course, and they were hooked, as were we all when we tried it. It became a family tradition that anyone going to Niagara Falls had to go to St. David for fudge, always bringing some back for Zaida.

How measure a life? I wish for all of us that like my dad, we have a long and full life, enjoy our grandchildren and even great grandchildren, and leave good memories behind.

##

This story was first published in Today's Seniors

Exit Laughing

Borrowed Hot Tub

by Gordon Gibb

If Murphy's Law dictates that something awful will happen at the worst possible time, Gordo's Law guarantees that such a catastrophe will unfold at your neighbor's house when they're not home.

Before leaving for a Spring Break holiday back in March, our neighbors two doors down asked us to keep an eye on their place. *And by all means,* they said, *feel free to use the hot tub while we're gone.* Somebody had to maintain chlorine levels to the required standards. The commissioned caretaker might as well enjoy the outdoor convenience, too.

Grateful for the opportunity, my wife and I walked over later in the week with a bottle of wine and the key and, making sure all was in order in the homeowner's absence, settled in for a relaxing soak on their rear deck, in the fashion to which we are accustomed. *Just for a few minutes,* we agreed.

Well, you know how it goes – a few minutes turn into several, then thirty. We were beyond 45 minutes and nudging a full hour. With the wine bottle drained, we finally went for our towels.

Is an hour too long to spend in water heated to 104 degrees Fahrenheit? Obviously I didn't think so. But I didn't have much chance to think about anything, because within a few seconds of getting to my feet I was off them again, having fainted dead away to the floor of the kitchen: unconscious, convulsing and in obvious distress.

There I lay, looking every bit the ghost-like misfit from any Tim Burton movie you care to name. My wife, at a loss for words, managed a call to 911 anyway and within seconds the ambulance arrived, with fire truck in tow.

Now, imagine this scene from the point of view of the neighborhood...

Family leaves for vacation. House is empty. Suddenly, emergency vehicles screech to a halt in front of empty house, flashers blazing, lighting up the night. Attendants rush in and emerge with unidentified man lying on stretcher, presumably an unlucky burglar who stubbed his toe in the dark while robbing the owners blind, and had the good sense to call himself an ambulance.

I regained consciousness just in time to see the emergency services crew rushing in, to find me sprawled on the floor, naked to the world.

It is here I should mention that I work in the electronic media in my home city. My name is practically a household word. I couldn't help but wonder, then, if the young female trainee was sizing up more than the situation at hand when she peered down at me and asked of no one in particular...

Is this the guy from the radio?

I had regained my senses by this time (if not my composure), and for the duration of my ride to the local hospital I kept thinking of poor old Gladys Kravitz, the nosy neighbor on TV whose mission in life was to peer out her window and spy on kooky neighbor Darin Stephens and his *Bewitching* wife, Samantha.

Lucky for me, newlyweds Shelly and Howie from across the road have too much interest in each other to be nosy. Their neighbor Bill has his office in the basement, and Reed is out doing something with the Kinsmen Club. But poor Susan, who just moved into the house between our home and our hot tub hosts two doors down, is new to the city and just beginning to size the neighborhood up. This can't look good.

My story, thankfully, has a happy ending.

After a few hours and some expert care at our regional health center, my plummeting blood pressure is reined safely into submission. I'm allowed to go home. Bill from across the way emerged from the bowels of his basement to greet us in our driveway. Susan has resisted all temptation to move away, Howie and Shelly were too busy getting pregnant to notice anything, and my wife later returned to the scene of the crime and dutifully cleaned up the splatter from my face-first swan dive into our neighbor's kitchen floor, while they were conveniently still away.

We continued our diligence with chlorination detail but deferred any opportunity for a repeat soak, and returned the key to the weary travelers a week later.

Welcome home, we said.

Thanks. So... how'd it go? Mmmmm?...

They were smiling from ear to ear. They knew. Somebody snitched.

Seriously, we're glad you're okay. And please feel free to use the hot tub anytime. But for gosh sakes, next time...

Please wear shorts...

##

This story was first published in the Peterborough Examiner

Crickets

by Barbara Florio-Graham

I don't have many fears. I'm not afraid of the water, heights, speaking in public, or snakes.

But I'm terrified of insects. My panic at seeing a spider is totally irrational and often hysterical.

So what am I doing with a cricket in my office?

My mother claims my fear of insects is inherited from her, but if that were true, why would my dread be so much worse than that of my sisters?

I do recall that all four of us, my mother, both sisters and I, were diligent in our Saturday morning efforts to keep our typical Cape Cod-style house free of cobwebs, and that Daddy was used to hearing a thin female voice, heightened in fear, summoning him from downstairs just as he sat down after supper to read the paper.

His muscled, weary body would trudge up the oak staircase, and, responding to a dumb gesture pointing to the corner where the ceiling joined the rose-papered wall, he would grasp the unsuspecting spider in his rough, automobile-mechanic's hands, as we covered our eyes and turned away.

So what am I doing with a cricket in my office?

Insects make me hysterical. When I was about six, one of my sisters, exasperated with my intrusion on her privacy in the room we shared, closed me inside, holding the door shut from the hallway, while whispering, *I just saw a spider in there!*

As my frantic eyes searched every corner, and my hands brushed my hair, my clothes, my arms, my legs, certain something was crawling on me, I heard her malicious giggle and I began to scream.

There was no spider, of course, which she confessed as soon as she realized that her prank was out of control, and I remember she was punished severely, although I was still so upset I took no relish in it.

But that still doesn't explain what I'm doing with a cricket in my office.

I didn't kill a spider myself until I was 25 years old and living in Chicago. I'd been told insects don't live in the higher floors of skyscrapers, and was reassured by the fact that my apartment was on the 42nd floor. But two months after I moved in I found a tiny black spider.

At first, I recoiled in panic, keeping my gaze fixed on the intruder so he couldn't slip into some crack to hide, where I'd have to endure forever the fear of his reappearance. Then I realized there was no Daddy downstairs to call, and I would either have to deal with the spider myself or watch, helplessly, as it crawled out of my sight to keep me awake for nights to come.

I stood transfixed, sweat beginning to soak my armpits and forehead. Slowly, I steadied myself against the dresser with my right hand and reached with my left for one of the slippers I knew were beside the bed.

Carefully transferring it to my right hand, as I was afraid if I missed, my courage would be for naught, I lifted the slipper and smashed the six-legged monster with all the force of my fear.

It left no mark on the windowsill, and just a tiny brown spot on the sole of the slipper, which I scraped off with a doubled tissue that I flushed down the toilet, shuddering all the while.

After I stopped shaking, I was proud of my accomplishment. Still, more than two decades after that triumph, I shiver every time I see an insect.

So what am I doing with a cricket in my office?

It happened by accident. A few years ago, when we were visiting my parents in Florida, my ex-husband caught two of those little lizards that are always crawling up the downspouts.

He managed to get them through Canada Customs, still squirming, and placed them in the smaller of our two terrariums, which happens to reside in my office.

The cat was delighted, and so was I, until my husband announced that all lizards, our geckos included, eat only live food. That meant insects! In my office!

The two as yet unnamed reptiles were banished to the basement, to live in the larger terrarium. The cat followed, and I heaved a sigh of relief.

Then, I heard a tiny chirping.

One of the crickets the lizards had dined on just moments before had found a hiding place, and now celebrated his escape with joyful sound.

My first instinct was to shout, *Peter*! in the same quavering voice with which I'd called, *Daddy*! years ago. But then I took a deep breath and thought about this brave young creature.

Was I going to condemn him to death after he'd miraculously defied the jaws of two hungry geckos? Wasn't it true that the Chinese considered a cricket in the house to be lucky?

I decided to keep the cricket, and call him Bravo.

Bravo called my office terrarium home. We realized that *he* was a *she* when two smaller crickets appeared. We called them Echo and Forte. They lived in a mini Eden, complete with jar-top dishes of cornmeal and water. I gave them pretty rocks and shells to climb on and hide under, and twice-weekly servings of lettuce to nibble.

They were very happy. So happy, in fact, that soon more tiny baby crickets began to appear.

Oops! When the cat was asleep, I carried the terrarium onto the front porch, removed the cover, turned it on its side, and allowed the crickets to escape.

Years later, when I open the front screen door in late August, the cat and I can hear the crickets singing.

It's not a bad sound, if you don't mind insects.

##

This story was first published in the Ottawa Citizen

Yours Without Compliments

by Lorri Benedik

Do you feel at ease expressing appreciation of other people's beauty, ability or taste? And how do you react when someone says you look marvelous or they love your hairdo or your new suede shoes?

If you're anything like me you find a subtle way to divert the attention. I tend to flail my arms wildly and blurt out something like, *Quick, look over there, isn't that a menacing squall line of cumulonimbus heading our way?* My method sometimes provides immediate temporary relief, but can occasionally make matters worse. If the focus is not successfully deflected, the perpetrator may be further impressed by my effortless command of sophisticated, multi-syllabic meteorological terminology. However, not too long ago I found out how much worse others are at taking a compliment gracefully.

A few weeks ago a neighbor dropped by our home to deliver the circulars she had kindly collected from our doorstep during a vacation. I said, *Sue, you look great, is that a new haircut?* She rolled her eyes, shook her head and replied, *My hair is filthy, don't even look at me, I am hideous.*

Then yesterday I met a new cashier at our neighborhood bank. I introduced myself, saying, *It's a pleasure to meet you. You have such a lovely smile.* She looked at me as if I was from Uranus, pulled the corner of her mouth open with a hooked index finger and mumbled, *Oh really, well take a look in here. I have a molar in back that is completely black.* Did I need to know that? And did she really have to show me?

But the clincher was the mom of one of the kids at my son's school. I hadn't seen her for several months during which time she had obviously lost a ton of weight. *Nina, I said, You look stunning! What's your secret?* Unfortunately, she took my question literally, replying, *I lost 70 pounds. You should see my breasts, They look like pita breads with nipples.* Since that day, try as I may to erase the mental image, she now plays the starring (not supporting) role in my newest recurring nightmare. I'll spare you the details, but let's just say that souvlaki and tzatziki are involved.

What is it about a compliment that makes us want to confess our worst sins?

Do we, perhaps, feel that if we acknowledge an attractive trait or two they will disappear? Are we fearful that there is a vigilant compliment monitor out there, just waiting for us to bask, for a blissful moment, in some positive feedback so that they can jump in? *OK, lady, step away from the Gucci bag, hands on the wall, no sudden moves.*

Or is it like Cinderella? Does the humble acceptance of kind words put us at four seconds to twelve on the night of the ball? Who wants her attractive new beau to turn back into Barry Manilow? (No offense, none taken). It has become so bad for me that I'm reluctant to order the special of the day if it comes with a complementary Caesar.

I'm also wondering if this disability might be a gender thing, Do men (other than metrosexuals, of course) have conversations that go like this?

> *Raoul, have you been working out? You're butt looks as firm as a rock.*
>
> *Oh Norbert, you noticed, it's actually not me, I'm a pig. It's my new control top briefs. Aren't they slimming?*

I'm unsure when, exactly, the challenge began for me. I know that as a kid I enjoyed praise from my parents and grandparents, which more often than not came with a reward in the form of sweets. *Lorri, you got another perfect spelling test. Have some chocolate, you good girl.* From that scenario I soon progressed to the self-managed feel-good reward system, which consists of sugary foods being consumed at every turn as a preventive remedy for the conditioned Pavlovian cravings that feeling good about one's accomplishments provokes. In layman's terms, the drooling begins immediately following the successful completion of the task and only stops after consuming a treat—or five. The compliment then becomes obsolete, having been usurped by the goody.

Guilt sets in immediately following the last chew. This process is on an endless loop. Do the math. Being a fatty is the inevitable result, which is great in a way, because it helps keep those pesky compliments down to a minimum. And, of course, if you lose the weight, some thoughtless clod will tell you that you look great, starting the whole need-for-a-treat cycle all over again.

The solution is simple, Be considerate—keep your stinking compliments to yourself. If you truly care for your life partner, try this at home:

Honey buns, do I look chunky in these capris?

Yes, my dumpling, you'd make a hippo look waifish.

Thanks, Angel, you always know just what to say.

##

This story was first published in Stitches

New Year, New Date

by Mark Kearney

Today's test. Please say the following historical years out loud–1492, 1776, and 1929.

Did you pronounce them fourteen ninety-two, seventeen seventy-six, and nineteen twenty-nine? Of course you did. If you didn't, then move on to another story in this anthology; we're done here.

Now say 2011 aloud.

You pronounced it *two thousand eleven* didn't you? I knew it.

Let me just state up front that I'm a man on a mission. We all need goals in life, and besides personally bringing peace and harmony to the world (I've pretty much got that sorted out), mine is to convince everyone that it's time to drop this *two thousand* thing and get on with what we should have been saying for years, which is *twenty-o-nine, twenty-ten etc.* Maybe it doesn't roll off your tongue as easily as two thousand (fill in whatever digits you choose), but it didn't stop you from saying *nineteen twenty-nine*, did it?

Now, if you were born in 1911, well, uhh, gee, congratulations on living so long. What's your secret? Anyway, if you're still around I bet you don't say I was born in *one thousand, nine hundred and eleven*. Or even *nineteen hundred and eleven* unless you just like to hog up airspace with the sound of your voice. It was always good ol' *nineteen-eleven*.

So, I think there are two reasons why people are still saying things like two thousand eleven or two thousand twelve instead of twenty-something. First of all, we had that whole millennium thing a decade ago when people couldn't simply just say *two thousand* but had to draw it out by saying *the year* two thousand. It was as if we were afraid we'd get it mixed up with *the price* two thousand or *the weight* two thousand or, I don't know, *the broccoli* two thousand. Even I, the champion of *twenty-eleven*, found myself saying it occasionally. It sounded better than *twenty hundred*. Or *twenty-ought-ought*, which is something you'd expect to hear from a robot in a B Grade sci-fi flick.

Speaking of sci-fi, we've also had to deal with Stanley Kubrick's movie from some 40 years ago, 2001: A Space Odyssey. Everyone said *two thousand and one* (there were also those people who couldn't pronounce the word *Odyssey* but I'm ignoring them), and it's stuck with us ever since.

So how do I convince you to switch from two thousand to twenty for the rest of this century? And don't tell me you're going to be saying *two thousand and thirty-one* another 20 years from now or I'll pick up my pronunciation handbook right now and go home. Fortunately, I've devised some simple exercises you can do in your spare time to help.

147

First, try counting from 15 to 25 each day. Try NOT to go *eighteen, nineteen, two thousand, two thousand and one...* Recite the old children's rhyme *five and twenty (not two thousand) blackbirds*. Yeah, now you're getting the hang of it.

Men, you'll like this next one. Get the TV remote and start channel surfing. Punch the keys to go from channel 20 to 11 and back, each time saying *I wonder what's on channel (fill in the blank)*. Repeat several times. I know channel 20 may have some lame shows, but give it a go anyway.

Seek out people with 20/20 vision and ask them about it. Gather with friends and play 20 Questions (it's much more fun than 2000 Questions). Multiply two times 10, or four times five, or even 6.25 times 3.2 and scream out your answer.

I realize it may take awhile to get used to saying all this properly, so perhaps I'll revisit this in a few more years to review your progress. Let's say we meet again in two thousand and fifteen.

Damn.

##

This story was first published in The Globe And Mail

Canada, Eh?

by Fred Desjardins

I am a Canadian. I was born 57 years ago in the Province of Nova Scotia, a place so unassuming that our unofficial motto is, *Well, SOMEBODY has to live here.* But for the tourists, on whom we depend for the lion's share of our income, we advertise it as *Canada's Ocean Playground.* The motto is even stamped on the license plates of our 1957 Chevies, luckless Ford Edsels, and college-student-powered rickshaws. And as a peninsula in the North Atlantic, we certainly have more than enough ocean to play in, unchecked man-eating shark population notwithstanding.

I must admit that it's a very pretty piece of real estate, marbled throughout with winding pathways, verdant forests, and reconstructed military forts dating from the 1776 American War of Independence from Britain. That story didn't have a happy ending for us for a long time as we were on the side of the Brits but our fealty was finally rewarded when The Beatles conquered America in 1964.

The old saying is that no matter how hard you try some people are going to hate you for reasons beyond your control. Well, that's true...unless you're Canadian. Canada is the world's mensch. No rogue states gearing up their nuclear capability to combat the *Canuck Peril*. No international terrorist groups occupying our embassies as metaphor for anti-imperialist angst.

In the world's eyes we're clean, friendly, impossibly fair, and a little goofy. Our national anthem, *O Canada*, pretty much tells the tale: A remarkably tame and uninspiring tune on a musical par with *Three Blind Mice* featuring lyrics that eschew the martial extremism of other anthems in favor of a clarion call to defend our borders by *standing on guard*, sans weapons, presumably armed with a bag of donuts and a double-double coffee provided by our national church, Tim Horton's Coffee Shop. Not surprisingly, we don't have a lot of murder (although we've taken nose-tweaking and hair-pulling to Olympian standards).

It's often said, particularly by my ex-wife, that size matters. And Canada is much larger than America. But 90% of our population is strung out, from coast to coast, within 100 miles of the American border. This is primarily because the rest of the country, ranging as far north as Santa's Workshop, consists of godforsaken permafrost moonscapes and glaciers stuffed to overflowing with the remains of dinosaurs, gold miners, and delusional 18th century adventurers trying to find the Northwest Passage to the Pacific Ocean in vessels barely equipped to ford an indoor swimming pool.

As a result our population is one-tenth of America's. In fact, there are more Texans than Canadians. A ratio that's on the verge of changing as capital punishment in that State seems to be a relentless growth industry. Few Texans taking that final walk along The Green Mile ever get a last-minute reprieve from the Governor, although I hear that some of them receive a bouquet of flowers and a hearty *Good Luck* from the state capitol as *parting gifts*.

For the many with just a casual awareness of Canada, it consists of our three *metropolises*, Vancouver, Toronto, Montreal, and little else. Not surprising as these cities constitute roughly 40 percent of the population of the country and house world class sports teams and music stars that scream international publicity. But trivia buffs and aficionados of the television show, *Jeopardy*, are aware of substantial communities in St. John's, Halifax, Moncton, Quebec City, Ottawa, Hamilton, Winnipeg, Regina, Calgary, Saskatoon, and Edmonton. Not that these folks are terribly interested in these places but you never know when a boatload of cash might be on the line for giving Alex Trebek (a Canadian, no less) the correct question.

What I find interesting is the number of Canadians who have become American and international icons without anyone knowing their lineage. Raymond Massey is the quintessential Abraham Lincoln, Raymond Burr is Perry Mason, William Shatner is Captain Kirk no matter how many funny commercials and TV shows he stars in, and Lorne Greene is forever Pa Cartwright.

We Canadians often lament that our greatest export is comedians. Apparently, Canada isn't particularly funny to Canadian comics but the rest of the world is a riot. And so we have Jim Carrey, Leslie Neilson, Martin Short, Rick Moranis, Catherine O'Hara, Mort Sahl, Howie Mandel, Dave Thomas, Russell Peters and a host of others offering up a collective whoopee cushion to the planet. On the other hand, for you math whizzes, since Canada has but a tenth of the audience of America then it makes perfect sense from a bank account perspective why these folks have taken the international highway. It must be deflating when 12 guys in mukluks show up for your performances, especially when you're paid in animal pelts. Not that that's necessarily a bad thing but the last thing I want is underwear woven from porcupine quills and a beaver tail tie festooned with alternately-flashing outdoor Christmas tree lights.

##

Cherry Season Again

by Steve Pitt

I have two cherry trees on my front lawn.

Right now, we're at the height of the harvest season. Tonight I am way, way up in my Bing Tree (named Bob) and although it is completely dark I can still see in the upper branches because my trees are right under a street lamp. The light helps to separate the good cherries from the ones the birds had half-eaten.

I am almost finished my picking when I see four teens on bicycles stealthily wheeling up the street. Just from the way they are skulking, I know they are on a scrumping raid, which is a yearly occurrence.

I'm not greedy but when it comes to my cherries I have one rule: if you want to pick some cherries you knock on my door and ask. Younger kids always do. The older ones tend to just do sneak raids because they're too cool to show manners. Worse, I often end up with broken branches and my cherries thrown all over the street.

Anyway, these kids park their bikes about two houses down and then crouch-creep up to my trees like baggy-pants ninjas. No knock on the door and *Pretty please, sir.* They are definitely doing the ole grab and run. I give them

about 30 seconds of undisturbed crime before I start
whipping rotten cherries at them.

> *Ow. Something hit me.*
> *Shut up. Someone will hear.*
> *Ow. I just got hit too.*
> *Ow. Who's throwing cherries?*
> *No one. Shut up.*
> *Bull@#@. Ow!*

It only takes about a dozen bops with cherry pellets before
they all decide to look up at once. With the street light
behind me, all they can see is the huge black silhouette of
something swinging down at them through the branches,
screeching

> *AAUUUUUUUUUUUUUUUUUU*
> *WUG-WUG-WUG-WUUUUGH!*

while shaking its fleshy jowls.

They are so terrified they forget how to ride a bicycle.
Instead, they grab their trusty mounts and run beside them
until they round the corner at the end of the street.

No bad deed goes unrewarded, however, I begin laughing
so hard I fall the last six feet out of Bob da la Bing and land
flat on my backside, Don't spill a cherry from my bowl,
though. I am also now the proud owner of a nearly new
size 12 left basketball shoe, a Nike, no less, because one of
those four kids takes off so fast, he leaves a shoe behind.

So tonight, while my butt sits on an ice pack, Der Uberhund, my huge mutt, is stretched out on her doggie-bed, elegantly holding the shoe between her front paws while rapturously gnawing it apart with her huge teeth. When she is finished I will put the shoe back out under the tree. Hopefully the owner will reclaim it and when he sees the teeth marks, he and his friends will try to imagine what sort of fat bottomed big toothed evil lurks in my cherry trees.

da-shadow-knowspitt

##

Double-Breasted Danger

by Debbie Gamble

Ever since puberty, I've had a dream. I dream that, some day, I'll drop a morsel of food as I'm eating, and it will hit the floor, instead of landing on my bust. Practically every blouse I own is marred by a food stain of SOME sort, all because my *frontal property* is the size of a subdivision, instead of a single family unit.

You've heard that old joke: *What's the height of embarrassment for a woman? Putting her bra on backwards, and finding out it fits better.* That has never been my problem, being one of those women to whom Mother Nature was (overly) generous, a woman who has to wear a 23rd Psalm brassiere. (*My cup runneth over ...*).

When I was growing up as a tomboy, nothing prepared me for the embarrassment and self-consciousness that the protuberances of puberty would bring. As a girl-child used to just wearing a linder (now called a muscle shirt) under my blouse, I went to bed one night as flat as the floor, and woke up the next morning as a size B cup. Training bra, heck—I broke training before I even knew I was in the game!

As I grew, I .... well .... grew. Before I knew it, I was 16, a size 16, and had a bust that arrived everywhere half an hour before the rest of me. It also attracted gazes and gropings like a magnet attracts metal filings. To this day, I have a permanent crick in my back from the *duck and run* maneuver I developed from evading the ever-questing hands of a lecherous boss during my first real job.

High school years meant Phys Ed. I *hated* Phys Ed. There wasn't ANY game I could play where my appendages weren't a hindrance. Basketball? I'd invariably get a penalty for traveling, because the guest referee would think I'd concealed the ball in my bra.

Bowling? My backhand warmup was great; however, my right breast would impede my forward swing, knock the ball off it's intended trajectory, and I'd score a strike—in the alley next door.

Archery? Think about it. An archer's upper torso turns sideways to the target as she draws the bow. Pah-twang! SNAP!! By the time the archery session was over, my chest was like blueberry-ripple ice cream: one half white, one half purply-blue. (There was a valid reason why the fabled Amazonian women would cut off one breast!)

I was a horse fanatic from toddler-hood, and horseback riding presented a whole new set (no pun intended) of problems. A sedate walk was ok, but a bouncy, animated, up-and-down trot set bodies in motion that a less well-endowed girl would not experience. By the time I completed a 15 or 20 mile long-distance riding competition, I would have an incredibly sore back.... and two black eyes.

157

My riding instructor, a mere slip of a woman (so flat, she had two backs), very kindly told me one day during a lesson that I would be *more comfortable and perhaps perform better if I wore a sport bra for support. Great idea, Marla,* I retorted. *But does anyone make them in industrial strength?*

Perhaps SOME day, I'll be able to afford that breast reduction surgery I crave so badly, and future clothing purchases will be unmarred. I'll finally be able to *make a clean breast of it.*

##

Biographies

Elle Andra-Warner is the best-selling author of non-fiction books (including *David Thompson* and *Edmund Fitzgerald: The Legendary Great Lakes Shipwreck)* as well as a freelance journalist and photographer based in Thunder Bay. She specializes in travel, history, and business writing; her feature articles have appeared in publications around the world. Her website is http://www.andra-warner.com.

A freelancer for ten years, **Lorri Benedik** enjoys writing prose as well as light verse. Her byline has appeared in a wide variety of publications. Lorri recently shifted her focus from magazine and newspaper work to biography and memorial-writing. She lives in Montreal with her husband, son and mini-schnauzer. Contact her at lorri@lorribenedik.com.

Luigi Benetton focuses on demystifying the technology industry and the benefits it affords us. He has also written on topics as diverse as the business of law, fascinating large-scale construction projects and professional squash. His website is www.luigibenetton.com.

A freelance writer, **Lanny Boutin** has been published in numerous magazines, including *Canadian Living, Canadian Geographic, Homemakers, Your Health* and *Chatelaine.* Her books include *Titanic: The Canadian Connections, John Diefenbaker: The outsider who refused to quit, Mummies: All Wrapped Up* and *Building Faces.* Her web site is http://www.lannyboutin.com.

Joanne Carnegie describes herself as *a keen observer of the quirky little corners of the human soul, a celebrant of absurdity and desire.* She has published essays, humor pieces, and creative non-fiction, and is working on her first novel, a mystery set in Montreal. Find her at www.writers.ca.

Irene Davis has written on a wide variety of topics, from the anatomy of a convention to life as a grandparent. In 2006 she was awarded the Peter Gzowski Literacy Award of Merit for an article in *The Globe and Mail* on her experiences as a volunteer tutor in Adult Literacy. Irene also teaches a grammar course online, focusing on common problems. Despite a couple of lengthy sojourns in Timmins, Ontario, Toronto is and always has been home. Check Irene out at www.writers.ca.

Fred Desjardins has been a humorist for thirty years and continues to get paid for it. He has lived in Sidney Crosby's neighborhood for twenty of those years but has yet to meet the hockey hero. He suspects that the young superstar is too intimidated to ring his bell. You can find his Olympian biography at http://www.fdesjardins.com.

Barbara Florio-Graham has won awards for fiction, non-fiction, humor, and poetry, and has written for magazines and newspapers across North America. The author of *Five Fast Steps to Better Writing, Five Fast Steps to Low-Cost Publicity,* and *Mewsings/Musings,* Barbara also teaches writing online. Her website is www.SimonTeakettle.com.

Trudy Kelly Forsythe is an award-winning journalist whose first major assignment was a feature article about moose for a hunting-and-fishing magazine. Since then, she has written for periodicals, radio, the World Wide Web, government and corporate clients. She lives, writes and listens to the Rolling Stones in Hampton, NB. Her website is www.trudykellyforsythe.com.

Debbie Gamble's work has appeared in many different horse and motorcycle magazines: the *Evening Patriot, Northern Aquaculture, TV Guide, Atlantic Books Today* and more. Her book about famous Canadian jumping horses, *Legendary Showjumpers*, was published in 2004; she has two more horse books in the works. Debbie lives in Prince Edward Island and writes about whatever piques her interest.

Gordon Gibb's work has appeared in *Chatelaine, Canadian Living, Maclean's, Cottage Life, Reader's Digest, The Globe and Mail, Toronto Star* and *Peterborough Examiner*. His book on Lester B. Pearson was published in 2006. Gordon does contract writing for www.LawyersandSettlements.com, Los Angeles. He is also a broadcaster and voice artist. His website is www.GordonGibb.com.

Helen Lammers-Helps is a freelance writer who lives near Kitchener, Ontario, with her husband and kids. She writes mostly about agriculture, food, gardening and the environment but will tackle just about any topic. To find out more, check out her profile at the Professional Writers Association of Canada (PWAC) website at www.writers.ca.

From being romanced on an ice road to running an alpaca farm in the Northwest Territories, **Hélèna Katz** has stories to share. She lives in Canada's North and has written for such magazines as *Canadian Geographic, Homemakers* and *Up Here*. She is the author of *The Mad Trapper, Gang Wars* and *Cold Cases*. Her website: www.katzcommunications.ca.

Mark Kearney is an award-winning journalist who has co-authored 10 books, including *The Great Canadian Trivia Book*. His work has appeared in some 80 magazines and newspapers in North America. Mark teaches writing and journalism at the University of Western Ontario and has won five University Student Council Teaching Awards of Excellence. His website is www.triviaguys.com.

Barbara Bunce Desmeules Massobrio, a native of Montreal, is a high school librarian who doubles as a freelance writer. She has written about topics as varied as: living in a Korean monastery, mixing drinks, and cuisine at the CIA. When not reading, writing or working, she travels. She shares her experiences at: www.travellingbooky.com.

Steve Pitt has been a freelance writer for more than three decades. He is the author of seven books and hundreds of magazine and newspaper articles. In 1980, he won a Periodical Distributors Authors' Award for humor for a *Harrowsmith* magazine article featuring gourmet groundhog recipes. His cooking has improved. His website is http://stevepitt.ca.

A professional photographer for 30 years, **John C. Watson** is based in Vancouver BC. His images have graced magazine and book covers, editorial pages, and creative advertisements around the world. John often works with his mother, freelance writer and author Julie V. Watson. The duo specialize in travel, food and nature, and also present workshops across Canada. For samples of John's work visit imps.ca.

Julie V. Watson is a prolific writer based in Prince Edward Island, or where their RV takes them, with 27 books and numerous articles to her credit. Her writing focuses on travel, food, lifestyles, seniors and entrepreneurship. She shares her passion for writing, POD publishing, photography and scrapbooking through workshops across Canada. www.seacroftpei.com or www.gotocreativeconnections.com

Hilda Young (Hon. B. A. History) has appeared in the *Winnipeg Free Press, The Cottager, Smart Connections, Faith Today, United Church Observer, Presbyterian Record, Christian Week, Cross Talk, Petawawa Post, Pembroke Observer* and *Ottawa Valley Business*. She is a member of The Word Guild. Her blog is http://hildaleapsforward.blogspot.com/

##

Other Titles Available From Bridgeross

My Life and Other Lies: Tales From the Writer's List, by Steve Pitt If you liked this book, you will like this one as well. A collection of stories from humorist Steve Pitt, described as "artful story-telling similar to the works of Garrison Keillor, the celebrated author of Lake Wobegone Days, and Jean Shepherd whose collected anecdotes eventually became the holiday classic A Christmas Story"

ISBN 978-0-98110037-7-7, $17.95 plus a Kindle sampler for only $2.99 on amazon

The Mysteries of David Laing Dawson - The Intern, Essondale, Slide in All Direction, and Don't Look Down Slide and Don't Look Down are new mysteries while The Intern and Essondale are trade paper reprints originally published by MacMillan. Dawson is a Hamilton, Ontario, psychiatrist whose mysteries have been translated into seven languages and who has been compared to Robin Cook. These titles are available in trade paper and in Kindle and other e-book formats.

The Adolescent Owner's Manual, by Dr. David Laing Dawson "Dawson's understated sense of humor translates well to text. While there are a plethora of books available on parenting teens, his to-the-pointness recommends this for busy readers." - Library Journal, ISBN 978-0-9866522-0-2, $15.95 in trade paper and also available in Kindle and other e-book formats

Mental Illness Titles:

Schizophrenia: Medicine's Mystery Society's Shame, by Marvin Ross
recommended by the World Fellowship for Schizophrenia and Allied
Disorders, ISBN 978-0-9810037-0-2, $19.95

After Her Brain Broke: Helping My Daughter Recovery Her Sanity,
by Susan Inman with an introduction by Senator Michael Kirby, Chair,
The Mental Health Commission of Canada, and recommended by the
National Alliance on Mental Illness (US), EUFAMI (Europe) and The
Mood Disorders Association of Canada, ISBN 978-0-9810037-8-8 , $18.95

My Schizophrenic Life: The Road To Recovery From Mental Illness,
by Sandra Yuen MacKay described as "compelling" by Library Journal
and recommended by The Mood Disorders Association of Canada.
ISBN 978-0-9810037-9-5, $19.95

CPSIA information can be obtained at www.ICGtesting.com

225371LV00001B/13/P